PURRFECT ZOO

THE MYSTERIES OF MAX 69

NIC SAINT

PURRFECT ZOO

The Mysteries of Max 69

Copyright © 2023 by Nic Saint

All rights reserved. No part of this book may be reproduced in any form by any electronic or mechanical means including photocopying, recording, or information storage and retrieval without permission in writing from the author.

This is a work of fiction. Names, characters, places, brands, media, and incidents are either the product of the author's imagination or are used fictitiously. The author acknowledges the trademarked status and trademark owners of various products referenced in this work of fiction, which have been used without permission. The publication/use of these trademarks is not authorized, associated with, or sponsored by the trademark owners.

Edited by Chereese Graves

www.nicsaint.com

Give feedback on the book at: info@nicsaint.com

facebook.com/nicsaintauthor
@nicsaintauthor

First Edition

Printed in the U.S.A

PURRFECT ZOO

Keeping up with the Pooles

It isn't often that a distant cousin you didn't even know existed decides to leave you five million dollars, so when Odelia's cousin Beatrice passed away, and was gracious enough to include Odelia in her will, it was the start of a new adventure for all of us. Because one of Cousin Beatrice's stipulations was that we should take over her Alaskan zoo, which housed no less than three hundred cats. And also, camera crews had to film the process. Which is how we became the stars of our own reality show, with cameras filming our every move.

This wouldn't have been such a big deal, if we didn't also have a triple homicide to solve. Three members of the same family had been killed, and the only witness to the crime had mysteriously disappeared without a trace. And since there was no evidence and plenty of suspects to choose from, we had our work cut out for us.

CHAPTER 1

Robert Ross looked down at the dog he was walking and wondered if he'd ever seen a finer specimen of the canine species. Marlin was perfectly proportioned, with the perfect type of fur, the perfect tawny color, and from the way he looked up at him, you could see that he was without a doubt the most intelligent dog that had ever lived. His gaze exuded smarts and just a hint of arrogance, which actually suited him well. Marlin had been his trusty canine companion for going on three years now, and Robert wouldn't have wanted it any other way. If he'd listened to Kimberly back when they'd first dropped by the pound to look at prospective candidates to fill the rather large shoes Marlin's predecessor Franklin had left, they would have taken a Chihuahua. "It fits so nicely on your lap," she had said. "And we can take it anywhere with us, even when we're traveling by plane."

But Robert had wandered off to look at some of the other canines while Kimberly stuck with the Chihuahua, asking the pound owner about a million questions. That's when he spotted Marlin, tucked away at the back of his cage, looking sad and forlorn. He didn't even respond when Robert crouched down in front of his cage and tried to engage the creature in conversation. Clearly, something traumatic had happened to the dog, and he had become locked in his own shell, retreating from the world.

For some reason, the dog had appealed to him in a big way, so he'd interrupted his wife's harangue and asked the pound owner about Marlin's history. It was the typical litany of being shifted from one owner to the next until the dog's proud spirit had been broken, and he had given up hope and belief that he'd ever find a true forever home.

That's when Robert decided to do just that. And so he'd taken Marlin home—funny name for a dog, but the pound owner didn't think it was wise to change his name now, since he was already used to it—against Kimberly's protestations, and he hadn't regretted it a single day.

It had taken a while for them to gain Marlin's trust, as the dog hadn't believed this could be it. That these people wouldn't return him to the pound after a couple of days, with a nasty case of buyer's remorse, but eventually he'd started to relax and become accustomed to his new home and his new humans. Pretty soon, Marlin and Robert had become inseparable, with Kimberly complaining that he seemed to like the damn dog more than her. But then Marlin was so loyal, so loving, and so giving it wasn't any wonder that Robert adored the creature, and in due course, the dog had also become fond of him, the man who had saved him from that dreadful fate back at the pound.

The dog barked once, and Robert knew exactly what that meant. He was ready to go to the dog park, to do his business but also to play with the other dogs while Robert chatted with the other dog owners.

And as they set foot and paw to the dog park, Robert

thought not for the first time that he may have saved the dog, but the dog had also saved him.

The dog park was pretty busy at this time of the morning, but he didn't mind. He knew most of the other people there, and by now Marlin knew most of the other dogs and got along with them very well indeed.

Robert let Marlin off his leash, and immediately the dog made a beeline for a small group of fellow canines. They were a big sheepdog answering to the name Rufus and a small Yorkie answering to the name Fifi, and he got along with those two particularly well for some reason.

Robert walked over to the dogs' respective owners: Ted Trapper and Kurt Mayfield, and the men greeted him with a curt nod of the head.

"Marlin is looking good today," said Ted, the most talkative of the duo.

"Yeah, he's been feeling good," he said with satisfaction. "I gave him some extra-juicy leftovers this morning, and he seemed to like it. He's had some tummy trouble the last couple of days, and the vet said we shouldn't feed him kibble for a while, only food straight from our table, and see if it makes a difference."

"If I gave Fifi food straight from the table," grunted Kurt Mayfield, "she'd be hopping all over our table all the time." He grinned. "I wouldn't mind, though. Once you've got a dog, there's nothing you wouldn't do for the furry creature, is there?"

"Yeah, isn't that just the case?" said Ted with a happy sigh. "Though I gotta admit, Marcie doesn't always feel the same way."

"Yeah, my girlfriend doesn't either," Kurt confessed. "She likes Fifi and tolerates her to some extent for my sake, but if she's totally honest, I think she wouldn't mind if she wasn't there."

"My wife had her doubts about Marlin," said Robert. "When we picked him up at the pound, she actually wanted to adopt a Chihuahua, but I managed to talk her into adopting Marlin instead. I mean, Chihuahuas are popular, and that dog would have been adopted by anyone, but Marlin was one of those rejects that nobody seemed to want. He kept being shifted back to the pound by the respective adoptive parents that took him in until he was so demoralized he just retreated into a world of his own. You should have seen him when I first laid eyes on him."

"And look at him now," said Kurt. "The happiest and liveliest dog in the dog park."

Robert watched as Marlin, Fifi, and Rufus played happily together, not a care in the world, and felt gratified once again that he had followed his intuition and decided to take a chance on the mutt. It was only fair since Marlin had to take a chance on his new pet parents. And it had worked out to their satisfaction — both human and dog.

He looked up where a sort of commotion alerted them that something was going down on the street side of the dog park.

"Who's that?" asked Robert, referring to an older lady who was passing by in the company of no less than four cats.

"Oh, that's Vesta Muffin," said Kurt. "She's my neighbor."

"Yeah, my next-door neighbor too," said Ted. "She's crazy but also nice."

"That describes her to a T," said Kurt with a grin. "The whole family is nice but crazy. And I've had to endure the presence of those four cats for a while now, and I gotta say, it hasn't always been easy. They have this habit of caterwauling in the middle of the night for some reason, and when I say something about it, Vesta gets upset, and so does the rest of the family."

"Crazy cat family, huh?" said Robert. He didn't mind. He

was crazy about Marlin, so he could understand that there were folks out there who were crazy about their cats. To each their own.

"The daughter works at the library," Kurt continued, "and is married to a doctor. Then there's the granddaughter who's a reporter and sometime amateur detective. She's married to a cop. And there's also a great-granddaughter who likes to toddle around the backyard and play with the cats."

Robert winced. "Isn't that awfully dangerous? I mean, cats and toddlers, that can't be a great combination, right?"

"Oh, no, it's fine," Ted assured him. "They're very well-behaved, those Poole cats. In fact..." He glanced over at Kurt, then quickly closed his mouth, as if he'd said something wrong.

"In fact, what?" asked Robert.

"Nothing," Ted said. "Oh, will you look at that? Our dogs and Vesta's cats are hanging out together. Isn't that cute?"

Robert eyed the strange scene with interest. It was true: their dogs and that old lady's cats did indeed seem to enjoy spending time together, which was unusual, he thought, since cats and dogs don't always get along.

"It's almost as if they're... talking to each other," he said.

Kurt and Ted shared another look, and he had a feeling there was something they weren't telling him.

"What?" he asked then. "What is it?"

Kurt shrugged. "It's just a rumor, but..."

"I don't believe it myself, to be honest," said Ted.

"Me neither," Kurt assured them.

"What rumor? What are you talking about?"

"Well, rumor has it that the three ladies—grandmother, daughter, and granddaughter—are able to communicate with their cats."

Robert waited for the punchline, but when it didn't come and the two men remained serious, he frowned. "But that's impossible. Humans can't communicate with cats, just like we can't communicate with dogs." Though wouldn't it be nice if he could? He sure would like to know what Marlin was thinking sometimes. And he wouldn't mind telling him what he was thinking.

"It's just a rumor," Ted said with a shrug. "I'm not sure if it's true."

"It can't be true," said Robert decidedly. "The laws of nature don't allow it. If all species had the ability to communicate with each other, that would mean we could talk to birds, to chickens, to... to ducks in the pond." He laughed. "It would be like living in a Disney movie!"

"Like Ted said," said Kurt. "It's just a crazy rumor. Frankly, I don't believe a word of it. Just gossip, you know. I mean, you know what people are like, especially in a small town like ours."

"Oh, I sure do," Robert said. He and Kimberly had only moved to Hampton Cove six months ago, and already Kimberly was regretting their decision, complaining that Hampton Cove was like a dead zone where nothing ever happened, and where the people weren't friendly to her. She claimed that when she went shopping, they simply ignored her, then started gossiping about her behind her back. Robert had suggested she join some clubs, but Kimberly said there weren't any, which he found hard to believe, since every town has clubs.

At least they had their jobs, which guaranteed some human interaction with their colleagues. And of course, there were Ted and Kurt at the dog park. Those guys had taken him in from the beginning and hadn't even looked down their noses at him even once. That was the beauty of being a dog owner: whether you lived in Hampton Cove, Albuquerque, or the moon, you always had something in common. Like a secret club you were all members of.

The cats seemed to have moved on, and the old lady disappeared around the corner. It seemed a little weird to Robert that she would be walking her cats, just like the rest of them walked their dogs, but then she probably was a little eccentric, if those rumors were circling around that she could talk to her cats. Maybe she did talk to her cats, and maybe she even believed that her cats talked back to her. But all in all, it was nonsense, of course, and the woman probably had a screw loose.

CHAPTER 2

"So who's the new guy talking to Ted and Kurt?" asked Brutus.

"Um... I think his name is Robert," said Gran. "He moved into the old Michaelson place down the street. That house that was totally run down? They've fixed it up nice, and now it's a real credit to the neighborhood. I haven't actually met them yet, but talk around the block is that the woman is really snooty. The guy is all right. Friendly with all the neighbors."

"He sure seemed friendly with Ted and Kurt," said Brutus. "But then he probably has to be if he wants to become part of our local community."

"It's not easy," said Gran. "Some of our neighbors aren't always as welcoming as they could be. They don't like newcomers, especially when they're not from around these parts and if they haven't lived here for at least ten generations."

Brutus laughed. "Ten generations!"

"Have you lived here ten generations, Gran?" asked Dooley.

Gran nodded. "I guess so. I've never actually tracked my pedigree, you know, but it wouldn't surprise me if my forebears arrived here many years ago and helped put this town on the map." She frowned. "I just hope that the Rosses will start to feel at home here. A community needs fresh blood. And I have to say, Ted and Kurt have some great things to say about Robert and Kimberly Ross. They're both schoolteachers, and by all accounts, they're both real popular with their students."

"Snooty or not, that's nice," said Max.

Vesta grinned at the big red cat. "Kids never think anyone is snooty, and I think that even if you are snooty, it's very difficult to be snooty with kids since they're so disarming and don't care what you wear or what you look like. They haven't been spoiled by the world yet."

"Like Grace?" asked Dooley.

Vesta nodded. "Yeah, exactly like Grace." She adored her great-granddaughter and thought she was just about the most gorgeous little treasure that had ever been put on this planet.

She quickly walked on, suddenly remembering the whole reason she had come out in the first place. "We better get a move on, you guys," she said, urging on her small clowder of cats. "We don't want to be late for our next visit."

She had been selected, along with a couple of other cat parents, to present an award to the best pet parent in Hampton Cove. It was a prestigious thing, and she was happy that they'd chosen her to give out the award, as organized by the Hampton Cove Pet Owners Society. All the pet parents in town were eligible to select candidates and award points. She would have selected her granddaughter, who she thought was simply wonderful with their cats, but that's not how the competition worked. You couldn't select members of your own family. Otherwise, everyone would do that, and nobody would get enough points to qualify for the big prize.

So over the course of the next couple of weeks, the members of the jury, of which Vesta was a member, had to pay a visit to the different pet parents and monitor their activities, interview them about their habits and their everyday life, and generally decide how well they were treating their pets and how happy those pets were. At first, Vesta had balked at the whole idea of pitting pet parents against one another, figuring there was no need for such an award. But after having spoken to the organizing committee and especially the chair of that committee, Marjorie Sooms, she understood that there was a reason they had decided to organize the competition. There had been rumors about people neglecting their pets and not treating them as well as they should. So this whole award business was an opportunity for them to discreetly take a closer look at some of the dynamics at play between pet and pet parent and possibly offer suggestions on how to improve that relationship. And if they happened to come across a flagrant case of neglect or even outright abuse, they'd notify the proper authorities, and they could launch an official inquiry and even remove the pet from that home.

It was a noble cause, and so Vesta had wholeheartedly given it her support.

Which is why she was now on her way to talk to just such a family. And because she couldn't talk to dogs herself, she had decided to take one of her cats along, knowing that they could talk to dogs and would alert her if there was anything out of the ordinary. But since she couldn't just pick one cat, since the others would feel neglected or left out, she had to take all four of them. It was a strange sight, but then as the official representative of the Hampton Cove Pet Owners Society, it wasn't unheard of for her to be accompanied by her own pets. People might look at her a little strange, but by now most of them knew that she often ventured out with her four fur-balls in tow, and so did her daughter and granddaughter.

They had arrived at their destination, and she applied her finger to the buzzer. When no response came, she glanced through the little window next to the door to see if she could spot the owner of the house.

"Strange," she said. "I confirmed our appointment last night."

"Maybe they're out back," Max said. "And can't hear the bell."

"I guess so," said Vesta. And since she didn't want to stand on that porch all day, she figured she might as well do a little harmless trespassing to see if Max's theory was correct.

The cats were already heading that way, and she followed. And it was when she arrived in the backyard that she saw it: the lady of the house was seated on the swing at the back of the garden, looking dead to the world. She smiled and headed over there. She knew that Chloe Fisher was a well-known interior designer, married to an ad exec, and they were the proud owners of a lovely little Bichon Frisé who answered to the name Bella. And it was Bella she now saw, seated at the feet of her mistress, and barking up a storm the moment they arrived on the scene. And she had just reached the duo when she saw, to her dismay, that Chloe still hadn't moved an inch. And as she reached out a hand to alert the woman of their presence, suddenly Chloe Fisher… dropped from the swing and fell to the floor.

Her eyes were open, but she was very obviously dead.

CHAPTER 3

I don't know if you've ever seen a dead person, but if you haven't, I can't say I'd recommend the experience. It's a little disconcerting, to say the least, and even though I have witnessed my fair share of the deceased, it never fails to give me the willies, to be honest. Especially as this particular person dropped right in front of me, causing me to gaze into her eyes for a moment before I finally managed to drag my attention away and look elsewhere.

We had come to the home of Mrs. Fisher with the express purpose of investigating a complaint we had heard that she had been mistreating her canine friend. But now it seemed clear that we'd arrived too late, for the person we were supposed to investigate under the guise of a visit from the Pet Owners Society was no longer with us.

Behind her sat the Bichon Frisé under consideration, and as we transferred our attention to the small white fluffy lapdog, it was clear that she wasn't taking too well to this sudden demise of her human.

"Bella, right?" asked Harriet, who was the first to recover

from the shock of discovering our hostess dead. "My name is Harriet, and these are my friends Max, Dooley and Brutus."

Bella simply stared at us, clearly very impressed with these recent shocking events that had visited her home.

"Give her some space," Brutus advised. "She's obviously had a great shock and probably is in need of a little breathing room to process what happened."

"Oh, I know what happened," said the doggie, speaking up for the first time. "In fact, I know exactly what happened, and..." Suddenly she performed a sort of impromptu jig on the spot. "And I'm so happy! So happy I could sing! Sing my little heart out! The witch is dead—the witch is dead, yippee!"

I think it's safe to say we all stared at the small lapdog with horror written all over our features. It was no way to behave in the face of the tragedy that had just befallen the dog. And I think Dooley said it best when he stated, "It's the shock. It's made her go mad, the poor thing."

"I'm not mad, I'm glad!" the doggie caroled happily. "This is the gladdest, happiest day of my whole life! The dragon has been slain, and I couldn't be happier!"

"Look, I'm all for the freedom of expression and all that," said Brutus, "but there are limits, Bella. Your human died, and you shouldn't celebrate. It's not done."

"Well, I'm doing it," said Bella. "And you can't stop me!" And to show us she wasn't kidding, she went skipping off in the direction of the house, singing a happy song all the while. And Brutus, as she had indicated, didn't stop her.

"Poor thing has gone completely crazy," said Harriet, shaking her head sadly.

"It's understandable," said Dooley. "If something were to happen to our humans, we would probably go a little crazy ourselves."

"Yeah, I guess so," said Brutus, who was staring after Bella as she passed through the pet flap and disappeared into the house. "But not so crazy we'd say a lot of very awful things about them. Calling the woman a witch. My God. After she probably starved herself so she could feed her dog. Maybe that's why she died, sacrificing herself for her precious pet."

"Maybe Bella wasn't all that fond of her human?" Dooley suggested finally, having given the matter some thought. "She did seem happy that she's dead."

But before we had a chance to go further into this peculiar example of the human-canine bond, Gran alerted us to the importance of keeping our wits about us and paying attention.

"I think she was murdered," our aged human now claimed. She had been taking a closer look at the dead woman and now straightened again.

"What makes you say that?" I asked.

"My main clue is the big butcher knife that's sticking out of her back."

We all moved to where Gran was pointing, and I saw she might just have a point. There was indeed a very large knife sticking out of the unfortunate Mrs. Chloe Fisher's back.

"That should do the trick," I agreed.

"Yeah, I don't think she put it there herself," Brutus indicated.

"Unless she fell from the swing and landed on top of the knife?" Dooley suggested, offering us an alternative view.

"She only fell off the swing after we arrived," Gran pointed out. "So she couldn't have fallen on that knife, Dooley. No, this woman was murdered, and if I'm not mistaken, it happened right before we arrived, so the murderer could still be in the area."

We all scanned the boxwood hedge that lined the backyard. Located behind the swing, it obscured the view of whatever was behind it, or whoever was hiding in there!

PURRFECT ZOO

"You better take a look," Gran suggested, and for some reason, she was looking at Harriet and Brutus as she said it.

"Why us!" Harriet cried indignantly.

"Probably because we spend most of our time in the bushes," Brutus grunted, and with hanging paws, he and Harriet did as they were told and disappeared into that hedge. A couple of breathless moments later, they returned empty-pawed.

"No sign of any murderer in there," said Brutus. "There is a fence, though, so maybe he scaled it after having done the dirty deed and is now escaping via the neighboring gardens."

Gran decided that now that the coast was clear, she might as well take a gander herself, and so she headed for that fence and hoisted herself up to take a look at those neighboring gardens Brutus had mentioned.

"Nothing doing!" she announced after a moment. "I see a nice garden, a barbecue set, a pool, but no murderer."

She sounded relieved as she said it. It's one thing to come upon a dead body, but another to come upon the person who made it so. The evil might not have expended itself yet, and the murderer just might turn his homicidal rage on the poor hapless witness!

Dooley must have followed the same line of thought, for he said, "I just hope he doesn't have more knives in his collection, Max." He shivered. "I don't think I would enjoy getting a knife planted in my back."

"No, I wouldn't either," I confessed.

Moments later, Gran was calling the police, and as she was relaying the facts of the case as they had presented themselves to us, I wondered where Mrs. Fisher's husband could be. The couple were supposed to meet us and talk to us together.

Gran must have asked herself the same question, for she now told the dispatcher, "And of the husband, there's no trace. So chances are that he's the killer." She listened for a moment. "Yeah, a big knife of the kitchen variety. The brand?" She glanced over at the hilt. "I'm sorry but I can't make out the brand since the knife has been shoved in all the way to the hilt. Yeah, all the way. Why?" She listened some more. "Yeah, I'm sure it must be a great quality knife, Dolores, nice and sharp. And I can understand how important it is for you to sample different brands for your big kitchen remodel that's coming up, but I'm not going to pull it out to check the brand on this one. You'll just have to ask the coroner when he gets here. Bye now."

She disconnected and shook her head. "I don't know if it's me, but Dolores seems to be going nuttier and nuttier."

"It's just you," Harriet assured her. "Dolores is a policewoman, so she's been dealing with murder all her life, making her jaded. We, on the other hand, are still pretty new at this, so we see it as a life-changing event, whereas to professionals like Dolores it's just one of those things."

It certainly seemed like a life-changing event to Chloe Fisher, I thought, as I overcame my natural aversion to dead people and studied the woman's body. Gran was right. That big knife would have done the trick. And as it had indeed been shoved in to the hilt, whoever the killer was must have used a lot of strength, for I didn't think it was easy to accomplish such a feat.

From the house, the sound of a doorbell sounded, and Gran shook her head. "I told Dolores the body was in the backyard, so why ring the front door?" But as she was heading for the house, suddenly a woman dressed in a red summer dress rounded the house, and when she saw us, hesitated for a moment before asking, "Is this Mike Fisher's house? It's just that I rang the bell but when no one answered I just figured..." She had now glanced behind us and saw the body, lying prone on the ground. The woman brought a distressed hand to her mouth and gasped in shock. "Is that... is she..."

"Dead," Gran confirmed. "No idea who made her that way, though. The police are on their way, so they should be here soon. Who are you, by the way?"

"Suzette," said the woman, still staring in horror and shock at the body. "Suzette Peters. I'm Mike's new colleague, and he told me to drop by so we could work on a project together."

"I haven't seen Mike, actually," said Gran, and now turned her attention to the house. "You don't think..." She glanced down at us, and I knew exactly what she was thinking.

"We're on it," I therefore announced and set paw for the house. We zipped through the pet flap Bella had disappeared through, and the four of us spread out to go in search of Mike, whose body just might be lying around somewhere, as dead as his wife. If Mike was supposed to be home, and Suzette's words seemed to confirm that, the killer might very well have murdered both members of the household, or maybe even more if the Fishers had kids.

It was a contingency I found very hard to take into consideration, but then you sometimes hear these stories about entire families being murdered. But try as we might, we didn't see any sign of another presence in the house, whether dead or alive, except for Bella, of course, who was in the kitchen eating from her bowl and didn't seem to have a care in the world.

So after confirming to Gran that Mr. Fisher was absent from the premises, I returned to the kitchen and took a seat next to Bella. "So about your human," I said.

She looked up, a happy smile on her face. "Isn't this the gladdest day of all, Max? The most wonderful day? The sun is out, the witch is dead, and all is right with the world!"

"About that," I said, deciding to broach the topic gently,

lest she suddenly snap out of whatever mood had taken her as a consequence of the shock of seeing her human being murdered in front of her own eyes, and attack me. "Did you see what happened just then? With the knife and the murderer and all?"

"Oh, no," she said immediately. "I know what you're doing, Max."

"You do? What am I doing?"

"You're trying to turn me into a witness to this crime. But I'm not going to do it. I'm not going to tell you who killed Chloe just so you can turn around and tell your human, who will tell the police, who will arrest the killer and put them in jail. No way. As far as I'm concerned, the killer did the world a great service, and should get a medal, not be punished with prison."

"You do realize that murdering people is generally frowned upon."

"I don't care. I laugh in the face of these artificial societal constructs, Max. I laugh in the face of justice being done. And I laugh at Chloe's killer and thank them, for they rescued me from a life of constant strife and turmoil."

"Chloe wasn't a nice person?" I ventured.

"Nice!" she scoffed. "She was horrible! Always shouting at me, and sometimes she would even pinch me, Max. Pinch me hard!"

"But why would she pinch you?"

"No reason at all! Just because she liked it! She was cruel, Max. Very cruel. And cruelest of all to Mike and to their daughter Allison, who could never do anything right."

"Did she pinch them also?"

"Oh, she did worse than that. She destroyed them with her tongue."

Dooley, who had joined us, now frowned. "How do you

destroy someone with your tongue, Bella? Unless she had a very long tongue that could lash out like a whip?"

"Words, Dooley," said Bella. "She destroyed people with words. She wasn't just physically violent, but she was also mean and cruel and could say the most horrible things."

"Okay, so where is Mike?" I asked. "And where is Allison?"

She gave me a keen look. "Now, wouldn't you like to know that?"

"Yeah, I would like to know that," I confirmed. "Because if what you're saying is true, then either Mike or Allison or both have just graduated to the position of prime suspect."

But if I had hoped this would cause Bella to give us a clue as to the whereabouts of Mike or Allison and whether either of them was Chloe's murderer, she wasn't giving an inch. "No way am I helping you guys capture Chloe's killer. Unless you want to give the person a medal."

"We could give them a medal," I said, "for the best arts and crafts made in prison."

She smiled a sly smile. "I think you'll find that you won't be able to break me, Max. I've been at the receiving end of so much verbal abuse that your words can't hurt me."

"I have no intention whatsoever of hurting you, Bella. But in polite society, murder is generally discouraged, and whoever perpetrates it is typically punished, otherwise everyone would start murdering each other with impunity. And we can't have that, now can we?"

"Oh, yes, we can," she said. "If the victim deserves to be murdered I think it's fine."

I decided that my attempts to get a witness statement out of her were in vain and decided to leave it for now. Dooley wasn't giving up so easily, though. "You can't really defend a murderer, Bella," he said. "Murder is wrong!"

"A social construct that I think you'll find isn't always

appropriate," she said, causing Dooley to goggle at her to some extent.

"But, but, but..."

"I know it's unusual to side with the murderer of one's own human," said Bella, "but in this case, I can assure you it's the only correct position to take, Dooley. And now if you'll excuse me, I have to head to the dog park to tell my friends the good news!"

And with these words, she was off, leaving us dumbfounded, flabbergasted, and even nonplussed!

CHAPTER 4

Cameron Brooks had just thrown his line into the lake and settled back when a distinct tug at the line told him that he'd already caught something. He hoped it would be a big one since his wife had been telling him that if he didn't come home with a nice big walleye, she'd start to wonder what he was doing out there by the lake all day. Ever since his retirement, Cameron had made fishing his main hobby, and it was true that he spent most of his days out by Lake Mario, weather permitting. It wasn't so much the fishing itself that gave him so much enjoyment as the peaceful atmosphere that reigned there. After having spent a lifetime as the CEO of one of the biggest shipping companies on the East Coast, he could use all the peace and quiet he could get. Stress had made the final years of his tenure as CEO so unbearable that he thought he'd probably need a couple of years of sitting by the lake to feel like himself again.

The tugging intensified, and his neighbor Joe Parker, who had been a regular at the lake for many years, yelled out, "Better reel her in, Cam. I can tell you caught a big one this time!"

"I sure did," he said and rolled up his sleeves, starting the arduous but also rewarding task of reeling in the big fish he'd caught. It didn't take him long to see its head break the surface, but when he took a closer look, it didn't look like a walleye at all. It looked like... a person!

Which is when Cameron Brooks abruptly let go of his rod and fell back on his tush. Looked like Mrs. Brooks would have to forego a nice seafood meal for dinner again tonight!

* * *

To say that Dooley was perplexed would be an understatement. In his mind, all pets should work together for the good of mankind, and one of those aspects was to make sure that there was less trouble and strife in the world, and most assuredly less crime. And so, if a pet blatantly refused, point-blank so to speak, to be instrumental in capturing a killer, like Bella had just done, it simply did not compute with the kind-hearted fluffy Ragamuffin.

"But why, Max?" he cried in dismay. "Why would she tell us that the killer should be rewarded? Even if Mrs. Fisher wasn't a nice person, she still didn't deserve to die, right?"

"No, if Mrs. Fisher not being a nice person was enough justification to murder her," I said, "then a lot of people are in the same boat. If Bella's reasoning were to become the norm, a lot of people would have to die."

"It's true," said Brutus. "There are a lot of annoying people in the world. But to go about murdering all of them seems a little harsh, Max."

We were in the backyard once more, watching as the crime scene people were investigating Mrs. Fisher's body, with police detectives combing the scene for clues as to the identity of the perpetrator of this heinous crime. Our own humans were there, of course: Odelia and Chase, and also

PURRFECT ZOO

Gran had decided to stick around. Chase was interviewing Suzette Peters, Mike's colleague who had chosen this exact time to pop round. Of Mike himself, there was still no trace, which made everybody very antsy indeed.

"I think the husband did it," said Harriet now. "It's always the husband, isn't it?"

"Unless it's the wife," Brutus pointed out.

I would have pointed out that Mike Fisher could very well be lying dead somewhere, a victim of the same killer, his body not as yet having been discovered. But then that would be speculating, and since we didn't have any clues as to what had happened there, I didn't want to muddy the waters with idle conjecture.

Odelia now approached us and gave me a sign that I was to follow her. I immediately traipsed after her as she traversed the backyard and entered the house through the back door. Once there, I saw that more police officers were going through the place, turning Mrs. and Mr. Fisher's lives inside out. That's the trouble when you're murdered: your privacy suddenly doesn't matter anymore, and people you've never met before start going through your personal stuff. I saw that one cop had gotten hold of Mrs. Fisher's phone and was now scrolling through it, eyes glued to the screen, while another cop was checking the contents of the fridge, sniffing at various food items to see if they could yield a clue as to what had happened to the woman, and a third cop was intently examining one of Bella's rubber balls.

Odelia had reached the front room, where the Fishers entertained their guests, and pointed to a spot on the carpet. It was a crimson spot, and it might very well be blood, though of course it could also have been jam.

I sniffed at the spot and determined that it was, indeed, blood.

"Could it be Mike's?" I asked.

Odelia glanced behind her, making sure that we were alone, then nodded. "My idea exactly. Either Mike is the killer, or he also was the victim of the same attack."

"But then where is his body?" I asked. I pointed to the spot of blood. "If this is Mike, that would indicate that he was attacked in this very room, before his wife was stabbed to death outside. But then where is he?"

"Beats me," Odelia confessed. "Unless he wasn't killed but merely wounded and decided to go into hiding."

"Or maybe he was so severely wounded he managed to drag himself away, but then collapsed somewhere and is breathing his last breath as we speak."

We shared a look of horror. Immediately, Odelia sprang to life. Her eyes scanning the floor, she searched for a possible direction Mike could have gone in, then enlisted my assistance.

"I just wish that Bella was here," I lamented. "Dogs are so much better equipped for this than cats are."

"Who's Bella?" asked Odelia.

"The Fishers' Bichon Frisé. She's very upset with Chloe, apparently, and even though she practically admitted that she saw the murder and knows the identity of the killer, she refused to help us. She said Chloe Fisher was a horrible person and she deserved to be murdered."

Odelia looked up at this. "She actually said that?"

"Worse," I said. "She said she was going to celebrate Chloe's murder and tell all of her friends that the witch was dead and that today was the happiest day of her life."

"God," said Odelia. "Imagine your pet being glad you're dead. She must have been a real piece of work, this Chloe Fisher."

I had managed to trace the little droplets of blood on the carpet all the way to the front door, and Odelia now opened it. Together we followed the trail and soon found ourselves crossing the street, where the trail continued through the front yard of the Fishers' neighbor, then behind the house, through the backyard, and finally, it stopped in front of the garden house located at the bottom of the garden.

We shared another look, and Odelia took a deep breath, then opened the door of the garden house. Since it was pretty dark in there, it took us a while to determine its contents. But it didn't take us long to discover Mike Fisher, lying on the floor, covered and surrounded by gardening tools that seemed to have fallen from the rack. One of these gardening tools was sticking out of his chest. It looked like garden shears, and as we approached, it didn't take us long to determine that, just like his wife, Mike Fisher was not of this world anymore and had passed beyond the veil.

"I wonder what happened here," said Odelia as she studied the mess.

"Either he accidentally dragged all of those tools down from the walls of the shed," I said, "or..."

"Or the same person who killed his wife also caught up with Mike and killed him," Odelia finished the thought.

But since it was hard to determine at a glance the exact circumstances of the man's demise, Odelia decided to guard the scene while she placed a quick call to her husband, who was still in the house across the street. Moments later, the burly detective came hurrying over, and when he saw the devastation and also the dead man, he cursed under his breath. "Christ," he said. "The hits just keep on coming."

"Do you think he was murdered?" asked Odelia.

"I'd say he was. Unless of course those shears accidentally fell on top of him and landed in that exact spot and managed to kill him. But I'd call that highly unlikely."

"Yeah, looks like Mike encountered the killer back at the house, in the front room where Max and I found a small pool of blood. Then Mike managed to escape, tried to hide in there, but the killer caught up with him. There was a struggle, causing all of these tools to become scattered about. But then in the end, the killer managed to finish off his victim by planting those shears into his chest."

"I'll get Abe over here," said Chase, referring to the county coroner, who was busy across the street but now would have to assign a part of his team to work on this second crime scene.

Dooley, Brutus, and Harriet had also caught up now and were glancing into the garden house.

"Another murder!" Dooley cried. "What's going on, Max?"

"I'll bet Bella knows more about this," Brutus grunted.

"Maybe we should pay her a visit at the dog park," Harriet suggested. "That way we could put some pressure on her to finally tell us what she saw."

Harriet was right. It was simply intolerable that we would have such an excellent witness, and she wasn't talking. Though from what I'd seen and heard of Bella, I didn't think pressure would do the trick. If anything, it might make her clam up even more. But then, since I didn't have any other ideas, I agreed that we needed to do something since she was our best witness so far. Or better yet, our only witness.

So I told Odelia about Harriet's suggestion, and she said we should go after the Bichon Frisé and do what we thought was necessary to make her spill the beans.

Which is why, five minutes later, the four of us traversed the streets of our town in the direction of that same dog park we had passed with Gran not all that long ago.

We arrived there in due course, and much to our surprise, we didn't see any sign of Bella.

"She did tell you she was coming here, right, Max?" asked Harriet.

"Absolutely," I said. "She wanted to celebrate the fact that her human was murdered with her friends."

But try as we might, we couldn't locate Bella. We did see two familiar dogs, though, the same ones we'd seen earlier: Rufus and Fifi. As before, they were accompanied by a new arrival in town in the form of Marlin. It was a little hard to determine what type of dog Marlin was exactly. He seemed to be a mix of a little bit of everything. In other words: a mutt. But even so, he seemed nice enough. And so while the dogs' humans stood shooting the breeze nearby, we decided to ask our friends if they had seen Bella.

"Haven't seen her," Rufus said. "And if I had, I would tell you, Max. I mean, murder?" He shook his head. "I can't imagine anything worse than someone murdering both your humans."

"A double homicide," said Fifi quietly. "That's terrible."

"And this Bella was celebrating?" asked Marlin.

"Yeah, she was very happy that her human was finally dead and said she was going to tell you guys all about it and celebrate."

"Maybe she got waylaid," Rufus suggested. "Dogs are easily distracted, you know. Well, at least this dog," he added with a grin, referring to himself. "I'll be heading in this direction, but then suddenly I'll see a nice bone, and I'll wonder whose bone it is, and then by the time I'm done sniffing the bone, I've totally forgotten what I was going to do."

"Same with me," Fifi confessed. "I get so easily distracted, it's painful. But then Kurt is also like that. Ever since he retired, it's almost as if he decided to take leave of his brain. After having been the most conscientious man all his life, retirement made him let go completely and wander through life half asleep most of the time."

It was an aspect of our neighbor's personality I hadn't seen yet, for Kurt always appeared very disciplined to me. But then Fifi probably knew best since she lived with the man.

"My human isn't like that," said Marlin as he threw admiring glances at the man in question. "He's the most disciplined man I've ever seen. Everything in the right place, his kitchen cupboards organized to within an inch of his life, also his garage and his study. Five types of kibble, all in separate plastic containers, with the names of the brand written on a sticker on the side, all arranged just so. It's amazing that some people can live like that. My previous owner—well, most of my previous owners, and I've had a lot, I can tell you —weren't like that. I wouldn't exactly call them slobs, but they were messy. Unorganized."

"You had a lot of different owners, Marlin?" asked Harriet.

"Oh, yes. About a dozen of them, I'd say. They took me into their home, then for some reason got annoyed with me and returned me to the pound. This went on for months and months until I finally figured I'd give up, and I would stay there forever, you know. But then suddenly Robert showed up and adopted me, against his wife's wishes, and life has never been so great. He adores me, and I adore him, and together we make a great team."

"At least you won't be over the moon if they murder him," Brutus said, causing Marlin to give him a look of horror.

"Please don't say that, Brutus. I'd hate for Robert to be murdered. He's the best human I've ever known, and I hope to be with him forever and ever and ever."

"Same here," I said. "We also love our humans to death and hope that nothing will ever happen to them."

"Which is why we need to convince Bella to give us the name of Chloe and Mike's killer," said Harriet. "So if you happen to see her, try to persuade her to come clean, all right? It's important. Because if this killer is some kind of pet-owner-murdering psychopath, your humans could be next. Or ours!"

CHAPTER 5

$\mathcal{B}$y the time we had returned to the Fisher place, Odelia and Chase were on the verge of leaving in Chase's squad car. When they spotted us, they urged us to hurry up and jump into the car, and the moment the door was closed, Chase stepped on it, and the car lurched forward, throwing us all against the backseat.

"What's going on?" I asked once I'd recovered my equilibrium.

"Yeah, why the big rush?" asked Harriet, slightly aggrieved since she hates getting her perfect fur mussed up.

"Another body's been found," Odelia announced grimly. "Fishermen dragged it out of Lake Mario."

"Oh, no," said Dooley. "Another member of the Fisher family?"

"I doubt it," said Odelia. "In fact, I doubt it has anything to do with the murders of the Fishers. This is probably completely unconnected." She sighed. "Imagine that. Three dead bodies in a single day."

"Tell me about it," Chase grunted as he sped through town on his way to the lake. He had activated his emergency lights

29

on the roof and his police siren, so we made pretty good time as we traversed the busy streets on our way to this third crime scene of the day.

"Abe Cornwall won't be happy," Brutus predicted.

"The victims won't be happy," Odelia pointed out, "that they've died."

She was right, of course. What is a little bit of extra work for the coroner and the detectives assigned to the case compared to the loss of lives?

We reached the lake shore in record time and saw a man dressed in a fishing outfit talking to a young police officer. The moment we joined them, Chase took over from the officer, who had been the first to arrive on the scene.

"Mr. Cameron Brooks discovered the body, sir," said the young officer.

"Do you come out here often, Mr. Brooks?" asked Chase.

"Most days," Mr. Brooks confirmed. "Ever since I retired, I like to come out here and fish, whether I catch something or not. Mostly I don't, but that's all right. I like the peace and tranquility of the place. Until now, of course." He glanced in the direction of a tarp that had been placed over what I could only assume was the body of the deceased person, and I could see from the expression on the man's face that the incident had greatly impressed him.

"In fact, I may never come here again," said Mr. Brooks. "My wife keeps asking me when I'm going to bring home a fish, but now I'll have to tell her I caught something entirely different instead." He gulped a little, and I saw that his face had turned a sickly green. He excused himself and hurried over to a nearby tree, where he proceeded to deposit the contents of his stomach against the innocent tree.

"He's been doing that a lot," the officer confided in us. "Looks like he's deeply impressed by what happened." He grinned. "But then members of the public aren't as used to all this death and decay as we are, sir."

"No, you've got that right," said Chase. "Nor should they be."

"Is it true that this is the third dead body this morning, detective?"

"Yeah, we just found a husband and wife on Stanwyck Street," said Chase. "And now this."

The officer now led us to the tarp and, with a sort of flourish, removed it, like a magician removes a sheet from the woman he's just cut in half. He seemed quietly excited about the whole situation, and I couldn't blame him. As a new recruit, he had probably been directing traffic until now. So to be assigned to his first murder case was probably a big step up in the world of policing. He was young, I saw, and presumably fresh from the police academy. And if I wasn't mistaken, he was also very eager to make his mark and earn his stripes.

Chase had crouched down next to the body, which was that of a young woman. In spite of the fact that presumably she had been submerged in water for a while, she looked well-preserved. A sad characteristic of humans floating in water for a considerable length of time is that they lose their good looks and start to resemble something from a zombie movie. Though instead of becoming part of the walking dead, the condition is more akin to the floating dead.

"Looks like she hasn't been in the water long," Chase determined, giving us the benefit of his expert opinion.

"Is this what they call a floater, sir?" asked the young recruit.

Chase glanced up at the kid and nodded. "It's not the technical term, but you're right. Floater is the popular term for what we've got here." He reached into the dead person's pocket and came away with a slim leather wallet, which he opened. A bank card had survived the assault of the elements, as it would, since we all know that plastic endures.

A quick intake of breath from Chase told us that he'd come upon something of significant importance. He looked up at his wife. "It's Allison Fisher," he said.

"No way," said Odelia.

"Way."

"Mike and Chloe Fisher's daughter," I told my friends.

"Oh, no!" said Dooley. "This is not a good day for the Fishers, Max!"

As Chase got in touch with Abe Cornwall, Odelia proceeded to interview Mr. Brooks, who had recovered from his ordeal sufficiently to talk about the harrowing experience.

"Poor girl," said Dooley as he regarded the remains from a safe distance, as if they could rear up and attack him. "She must've gone for a refreshing swim and drowned."

"Or she was murdered," Brutus opined. "Just like her mom and dad."

"I don't see a knife sticking out of her chest or back," Harriet pointed out.

"Let's wait and see what the coroner has to say," I suggested. "Often with these waterlogged bodies, it's hard to know at first glance how they ended up in that state. It takes a skilled coroner to determine the exact cause of death, so it might be a little while before we know what happened." And since we had our mission to accomplish in the form of a certain pet we had to find and interview, we decided to head back into town with Odelia. Chase would stick around until the coroner's team arrived and hitch a ride into town with them.

Moments later, we were in the car, and I think it's safe to say we weren't feeling all that well after our close encounter with a third dead person in the space of a single morning.

PURRFECT ZOO

Odelia dropped us off in town, where we would proceed to try and track down Bella, while she headed into the office to write up an article about the murders for the *Gazette*. She might be a police consultant, but she is also a reporter, so she had a job to do, and so did we.

Before long, we were traversing the streets of downtown Hampton Cove, hoping to find Bella and convince her to share with us what she saw that morning. Lacking other witnesses, she had now become a crucial eyewitness to the disturbing events as they had transpired.

So we popped in at the hair salon to ask Buster, our good friend who is usually very well informed, but he hadn't seen the Bichon Frisé that morning. Next was Kingman, whose owner runs the General Store, but he wasn't aware of any celebratory Bichon Frisé either. And as we asked around, talking to some of our other friends, nobody seemed to have seen Bella. It didn't take us long to come to the astounding conclusion that Bella had simply disappeared.

"It's okay, so we know she left her house to go to the dog park," said Harriet as we convened for a moment to decide on our next course of action. "But Rufus and Fifi and Marlin said she never showed up there. And we also know it's only a short trek from the dog park to Main Street, but she hasn't been seen here either. So basically," she said as she sagged a little, "Bella could be anywhere."

"She just lost her humans," said Brutus, "so she probably won't be feeling as happy as you claim she does, Max."

"Oh, but she was over the moon," I said. "Ecstatic. She said she was going to throw a party."

"It's true," Dooley confirmed. "She did look very happy."

"But then where could she be?" asked Harriet.

"Where do dogs go to party?" Brutus mused.

We all thought for a moment, but try as we might, we simply couldn't figure it out. So finally, we decided to give up for now. We had done everything we could to track down Bella, and there wasn't anything else we could do.

"She'll show up sooner or later," said Harriet, voicing a thought I'd had. "So let's just go home and await further developments."

"Or we could go to Odelia's office and see what else comes in as far as news is concerned," I suggested.

My friends all stared at me. "You don't mean..." said Brutus. "More bodies?"

I gave him a serious look. "At this point I wouldn't rule it out, Brutus."

CHAPTER 6

Kevin Thomson had been watching the goings-on across the street with keen attention. Ever since he'd installed himself in the small attic room of the house opposite the Poole place, he'd been experiencing one epiphany after another. As an avid reporter for the *New York Chronicle*, one of the lesser-known gutter rags, as they're called in the trade, he wasn't happy when his editor decided to send him out here to the sticks for a story he thought was as far-fetched as any he'd ever heard. Rumor had it that a reporter lived with her family in Hampton Cove, and the odd thing about this reporter was that she could talk to her cats.

When his editor had shown him the email, Kevin had obviously been skeptical. And then when that same editor announced he'd picked him to do a story on this cat-talking reporter, he told the guy he'd lost his mind. But since the editor was the boss, Kevin had finally been forced to acquiesce, which is why he now sat in that little attic room, a camera on a tripod positioned in front of the attic window, scoping out the place and the family that lived there.

And he had to say that his results so far had exceeded his

expectations and then some. Not only did this Odelia Kingsley appear to be talking to her cats on a regular basis, but also the grandmother and the mother. The only ones who didn't seem to engage in this weird voodoo business were the male members of the family, Doctor Poole and the reporter's husband Chase Kingsley. Apparently, they didn't possess this strange knack.

Of course, he didn't know if they actually *were* talking to these cats, only that it *appeared* as if they did. So he'd told his editor, who said he needed to collect solid evidence if they were going to print a story about it. He had to prove beyond a doubt that was what was going on.

Which was easier said than done, for how do you prove the impossible? But Kevin was nothing if not resourceful, and so he had devised his own way of getting what he needed for the story. He just hoped the cop wouldn't find out, or there would be hell to pay. The guy looked as if he wouldn't take kindly to anyone messing with his family, and he didn't blame him. They had a daughter to protect, and if this story about a family of weirdo cat-talking locals went public, their lives would probably never be the same again, as every network across the country, or maybe even the world, would send a crew down to Hampton Cove to park themselves on the couple's front lawn and make their lives miserable.

But since Kevin didn't have any qualms as far as the consequences of his work were concerned, he didn't mind all that much about all of that. What he did care about was breaking a great story and, in so doing, furthering his own career. And so he checked if all of his systems were a go, and walked down the stairs of the house where he was staying. The old lady he was renting the room from thought he was an FBI agent working undercover to catch a couple of crooks. If she knew he was, in fact, a reporter about to break the most amazing story that had ever hit their small town, possibly she would have kicked him out a long time ago.

* * *

Vesta had arrived home after the shocking events that had marred her morning. Instead of saving the life of a dog, she had witnessed the end of the life of one of its owners. It wasn't exactly the kind of thing she had expected when she joined her local Pet Owners Society to award prizes and catch pet abusers, but that's life in Hampton Cove for you: you never knew what was going to happen next. It was odd, she sometimes felt, that their small town would be so rife with murder and mayhem. Maybe it was something in the water. But whatever the case may be, she was glad she didn't have to solve this particular case and could hand it over to Odelia and Odelia's husband, who she was sure had the case well in hand.

And she was just walking up to the front door when a man approached her, looking a little trepidatious.

"Yes, what can I do for you?" she asked as she halted, her key held out as she was about to insert it into the lock.

"Oh, I was hoping you could help me," said the man, who was handsome to a degree, she thought. "I'm looking for Odelia Poole?"

"Lives next door," said Vesta curtly. Of course, the guy would be looking for her granddaughter. Ageism was an affliction a lot of people suffered from, and clearly this fella did too. "Though she goes by her married name of Kingsley now," she added for good measure, making it perfectly clear that whatever this fellow's intentions were, he better curb his excitement because Odelia was a married woman.

"Oh, I'm so glad I found her," said the man. "Are you related to her, by any chance?"

"I'm her grandmother," said Vesta, and made to enter the house. She had better things to do than to stand there chatting with one of her granddaughter's admirers, after all.

"I have some great news for her," said the man. "My name is Sammie Paston, and I'm a lawyer representing your granddaughter's cousin Beatrice, who has recently passed away in Alaska. She left Mrs. Kingsley a substantial sum in her last will and testament and appointed me executor of her estate. Mrs. Kingsley wouldn't be home, by any chance?"

At the mention of a substantial sum, Vesta pricked up her ears. "She's not home, but if you like, I can call her and tell her to come immediately. Who's this Beatrice you're talking about?"

"She was a distant cousin of Mrs. Kingsley's."

"Never heard of her."

"Very, very distant."

"How was she related?"

"As I understood, she was the daughter of one of Mrs. Kingsley's grandfather's cousins."

"Father's side or mother's side?"

"Her father's side."

"Mh, I don't know the Pooles all that well," Vesta admitted. "I know Grandpa Poole was certifiable, and so was Grandma Poole, so it's definitely possible they had a cousin who decided to go and live in Alaska, of all places. So how much?"

"Pardon?"

"How much money did this cousin leave my granddaughter?"

"I'm afraid I'm not at liberty to discuss these matters with anyone other than Mrs. Kingsley," said Mr. Paston.

"I should have known you were one of those," Vesta muttered darkly. "Okay, fine. I'll call her and let her know. Come on in."

And so, even though it was against her habit, she ushered Sammie Paston into the house and asked him to take a seat in the front room. It was where they were supposed to entertain guests, which didn't happen all that often since most people preferred the kitchen or the living room. Then again, she couldn't very well ask this fella to wait in the kitchen. Now, what kind of an impression would that give? He might decide to cancel the whole inheritance thing altogether and hold on to that money himself. After all, Mr. Paston was a lawyer, and as everyone knows, lawyers can't be trusted, what with their forked tongues and all.

Moments later, she had closed the kitchen door and was in communication with her granddaughter.

"There's this fella here," she told her, "who says he's handling an inheritance from your cousin Beatrice."

"Who?"

"Cousin Beatrice. Supposed to be the daughter of one of Grandpa Poole's cousins."

Odelia was quiet, obviously trying to construct her family tree in her mind and failing.

"Just come home, will you? The guy says Cousin Beatrice left you a substantial sum. I've asked him to wait in the front room, so you better hurry before he gets tired of waiting and skedaddles."

"But I'm in the middle of this article about the murders."

"What is more important, honey? Some dead people, or your future?"

"Oh, fine, I'll be there. Though I honestly don't remember having a cousin Beatrice."

"She lived in Alaska, so that's probably why you never heard of her. I mean, who in their right mind lives in Alaska, of all places? Surrounded by polar bears and freezing their nuts off."

She hung up after Odelia had assured her she would leave

straight away and would be home in ten minutes, max. Which reminded her: where was Max? And where were the others? But then, since they usually liked spending time hanging out with their friends in town, she figured they had probably gone to do that.

Odelia was true to her word: ten minutes later, she walked into the kitchen. Vesta had already brought the guy a tray with freshly brewed coffee and homemade cookies, and both had seemed to his liking, for he made no attempts to leave. And so, by the time Odelia finally arrived, she said, "I've been buttering him up. I think he's ready for you now."

Odelia laughed. "What did you do to him?"

"Poured him full of coffee and stuffed him with your mom's cookies. Now go, honey, before he goes back to Alaska and takes your money!"

She followed on her tiptoes as her granddaughter went to meet the lawyer and placed her ear to the door, listening carefully as their future was being decided in there. Even though by all accounts the family was doing okay, with no less than four breadwinners and one making a little extra by assisting her son-in-law at his doctor's office, it never hurt to add a little something to the pile. They might buy a nice, fancy place outside of town, maybe on that Billionaire Lane where all the fat cats lived.

* * *

ODELIA FELT that she really didn't have time for this. With no less than two murders and one possibly suspicious death on their plate, she and her husband had their work cut out for them. In fact, she had planned to quickly type out that article before heading down to the police station to discuss the case with Chase and her uncle. But her grandmother was right. If Mr. Paston had come all the way from Alaska to handle this inheritance, she couldn't ignore him.

"Odelia Kingsley?" asked the man as he got up from the armchair.

"That's right," she said, shaking the man's hand. "So what's all this about a cousin Beatrice who died?"

"As I explained to your grandmother," said Mr. Paston, who was handsome and courteous to a fault, "Beatrice Morris left you a substantial sum of money. And now it is up to me to make all the arrangements so you can be placed in possession of the funds."

"Is it a lot?" she asked.

"Five million dollars," said the man, making Odelia's head spin for a moment. Beyond the door of the front room, she heard a banging sound, and she had the impression that Gran had just fallen over and hit the floor. She couldn't blame her. Five million is a lot of money.

"I'm afraid I've never heard of a cousin Beatrice before," she said, hoping this wasn't a case of mistaken identity. It happened, and if that was the case, this man had come all this way out there for nothing.

"That's perfectly understandable," said the lawyer. "Your cousin Beatrice lived a solitary life and didn't have a lot of contact with the rest of the family."

"But why did she leave all of that money to me if we've never even met before?"

"Well, the thing you have to understand about Beatrice Morris is that she was a great patron of pets, more specifically of the feline inclination. She operated a small feline zoo at her home and also supported several initiatives to get stray cats off the street and provide them with a good home. And since you're quite well-known as a great supporter of cats yourself..."

"Well, it's true that I have cats," she said. "And that my

grandmother supports our local pet shelter. But I wouldn't have thought that my reputation as a cat parent would have spread as far as Alaska."

"It did," Sammie Paston assured her. "Your cousin Beatrice had been following your work for many years. She was an avid reader of your articles, especially those where you mention your cats, and she felt you were a kindred spirit. Hence the legacy. Which does come with one minor stipulation."

"Stipulation?"

"Yes. Beatrice felt that it was important that her work be continued, so she hoped you would pick up the baton, so to speak, and manage the small zoo she set up over the years."

Odelia gaped at the man. "You want me to fly out to Alaska and manage a zoo?"

"Well, no," he said. "The idea was that the zoo would come to you. Let me explain," he added quickly when Odelia opened her mouth to protest. "Beatrice had taken in many cats, all of whom had become attached to her to a great extent. So she felt that if someone took over from her, it should be a person who felt the same way about pets in general, and cats in particular."

"How many?" asked Odelia, her throat having gone a little dry.

"Three hundred, give or take," said the man in amiable tones.

"Three hundred cats!"

"That's right. And so Beatrice had arranged that all of them would be transferred here to Hampton Cove, where you could take care of them the way she had done all of those years."

"But I don't have the space to take care of three hundred cats!" Odelia cried.

"There's no need," Mr. Paston said, waving a reassuring

hand. "Cousin Beatrice has taken care of everything. She had acquired a small plot of land on which she planned to build a small sanctuary where her cats could live out their lives in perfect peace and happiness, looked after by you, her personal role model."

There were a lot of things Odelia wanted to say in response to that, but oddly enough, no words would form. So she opened and closed her mouth a couple of times, at which point the emissary Cousin Beatrice had sent across the grave gave her a radiant smile, interpreting her silence as approval, and said, "I knew you'd be thrilled by the news, Mrs. Kingsley!"

CHAPTER 7

We arrived at Odelia's office only to discover that she wasn't there. And as we stood around her office for a moment, wondering how to proceed, her editor, Dan, swept in, saw us looking quite forlorn, and said in that avuncular way of his, "Oh, if you're looking for Odelia, she was called away. Something about an inheritance from a distant cousin?"

"So she went home?" I asked, knowing full well the editor probably couldn't understand me but giving it a shot anyway.

Dan Goory looked at me, his white beard waggling in the breeze from the window that was open to let in some air, then he grinned. "You know, it's quite remarkable that Odelia can understand you guys, 'cause I sure can't. But good for her. So now I'm guessing you've just asked me a question, and if I think this through logically, it can only be that you want me to give you her exact whereabouts. Which is home, since that's where her grandmother called her from, and it's where this lawyer fellow from Alaska was waiting for her."

"Thank you, Dan," I said warmly.

"No, thank you, Max," he said, quite surprisingly, I might

add. "If it wasn't for you, Odelia wouldn't be the reporter that she is, and if not for Odelia, I wouldn't have the number of subscribers and readers that I have. So thank you, and I hope you will keep feeding us news hot from the griddle for many years to come." And with these words, he paid us a two-fingered salute, then walked out of the office with a spring in his step.

We watched him leave with not a little bit of wonder. "How did he understand what you were saying, Max?" asked Dooley.

"What I want to know is how does he know that Odelia can talk to us?!" Harriet said.

"I guess Odelia hasn't been as good at hiding her special skill as she thought she was," I said. "And as far as Dan understanding me is concerned, I don't think he does understand us, Dooley. But obviously he's very good at interpreting our meaning, which is what he just did."

And quite accurately, too, for he had answered the exact question we had been asking.

And so we returned home, hoping to find our human and await further instructions in regards to the three murders that had landed on our plate that morning. Well, at least one murder that we knew for sure since Mike Fisher could just as well have been the victim of a freak accident whereby a sharp and pointy gardening tool had lodged itself in his chest. And Allison Fisher could have died an accidental death by drowning.

We arrived home to find both Gran and Odelia seated at the kitchen table, both in quite a tizzy. The man from Alaska had left, but clearly his message had not been well received.

"He wants us to open a zoo!" Gran was yelling. "A freaking zoo!"

"Three hundred cats, Max," Odelia said. "He wants us to

adopt three hundred cats and keep them at this new zoo he wants us to open."

"*He* doesn't want us to open a zoo," Gran pointed out. "Your cousin Beatrice does!"

"I don't even know this cousin Beatrice," Odelia confessed. "I've never heard of her before. And now she wants me to adopt three hundred cats."

"And if you refuse?" asked Harriet.

"Then we can kiss that five million goodbye," said Gran.

"Five million? Cousin Beatrice left you five million?" asked Brutus.

Odelia nodded. "But only if I continue operating her zoo, which she was planning to ship over to Hampton Cove. She already bought the land and had arranged for the transfer of the cats by airplane. So now all we have to do is sign off on the thing and we're all set."

"Over my dead body!" Gran yelled, shaking a bony fist.

"So you really want to say no to that inheritance?" asked Odelia.

"Absolutely!"

"So no five million?"

Gran closed her mouth with a resounding click of her dentures. "My God," she said after a moment's reflection. "I want to say no, but... five million dollars, honey. Five million!"

"I know," said Odelia miserably.

Dooley turned to me. "See, Max? Money doesn't make you happy. Five million dollars and both Odelia and Gran are very unhappy."

"They're not unhappy about the money," said Harriet. "They're unhappy that they have to adopt three hundred cats to get that money."

"Three hundred cats is a lot," Brutus said.

"Why can't they simply stay in Alaska?" asked Harriet.

"Because then I would have to move there!" said Odelia.

"Yeah, that doesn't sound like such a good idea," said Harriet after a moment.

All in all, it wasn't a nice prospect, though it could have been worse, of course. It could have been three hundred dogs. Cats, we could handle. Dogs, not so much. But to Odelia, it clearly didn't matter what pets she would have to house at this new zoo of hers. Cats or dogs or kangaroos, she wasn't happy about this interruption of her routine and the addition of a huge responsibility she had never asked for.

"There's more," Odelia now revealed to us, looking even more miserable than before.

"More?" I said. "What could be more?"

"Cousin Beatrice loved her cats so much she wanted to focus the attention of the world on their plight. And the only way she could think of how to do it was by creating a reality show. And since she was too old to do it herself, and also she didn't think people would be all that interested in watching a reality show about an elderly lady who lived out in the middle of nowhere with three hundred cats, she figured we should do it."

We all stared at her for a moment, then Harriet said in a sort of jubilant voice, "A reality show?"

Odelia nodded. "So this Sammie Paston guy wants to install a ton of cameras here and next door and film the whole process of how we're going to open this cat zoo."

"Oh. My. God!" said Harriet, practically squealing with joy. "We're going to be famous, you guys! We're going to be like the Kardashians, but with cats! The Cat Kardashians!"

"'Keeping up with the Pooles,'" said Gran. "Though we could also call it 'Keeping up with the Muffins,' of course. Or possibly 'The Kingsleys,' though I think 'The Muffins' sounds a lot better. Has more commercial appeal, you know, since everybody loves a good muffin."

"Are you crazy!" Harriet cried. "It's going to be 'Keeping up with Harriet,' of course!"

"Oh, dear," I murmured. As if this murder business wasn't enough to contend with, now we were going to have to star in some silly show.

"What is a reality show, Max?" asked Dooley.

"It's a show where they film people in their day-to-day life, Dooley," I said.

"So they film you when you take a shower?"

"Well, maybe not."

"When you're brushing your teeth?"

"Not exactly."

"When you're in the toilet?"

"Um, no."

"I don't understand. Then when are they going to film you?"

"Well, probably when you look your best and are doing the kind of stuff you don't normally do. The kind of stuff people actually want to see, you know."

"Which is…"

"Oh, I don't know, maybe investigating a murder, like Odelia likes to do, or getting involved in a car chase, which is what Chase would probably be great at, or curing cancer, something Tex might be able to do. Though maybe not."

"Or singing the solo in cat choir," Harriet added.

"No," I said.

"Using my litter box?" Dooley suggested.

"I doubt it."

"Licking my butt," said Brutus.

"Now that might be interesting," I said. "For comic relief, you know."

Brutus frowned. "Licking my butt isn't funny, Max. It's necessary."

Odelia and Gran were still discussing the pros and cons

of accepting this inheritance and all the inconveniences that seemed to go with it, and at long last they decided that they were going to hold a family meeting and put it to a vote. If this happened, it was going to affect all of us—the entire family. So it was only fair that the whole family would decide. And since it was also going to affect the four of us, we would also get a say in the matter and also a vote.

"I'm voting in favor," said Harriet immediately. "And you guys are too!" she added for our benefit.

"I'm not sure," I began.

"Max, you're voting in favor of accepting the inheritance!" Harriet said emphatically and gave me a look of such vehemence I decided in the interest of my personal safety to go along with her on this. After all, I didn't want to wake up one morning to discover I was missing a part of my anatomy. Like my head, for instance.

And so it was decided: a family meeting would be held that night, and the matter thoroughly threshed out.

CHAPTER 8

Chase had his work cut out for him, with no less than three deaths to contend with. But if he thought that was the worst of his problems, he soon discovered he was mistaken. For when his wife dropped in unannounced and told him she was organizing a family meeting that night about some inheritance she was getting, and they had to decide whether to star in a reality show and open a zoo, it took him a moment to process all of that and remind himself he was fully awake and not starring in a dream—or a nightmare.

"You have got to be kidding," he said therefore.

"No, I'm not. My cousin Beatrice died, and she left me her zoo. She also left me five million dollars, but only if we accept to open and operate this zoo and allow a camera crew to capture every moment of it."

"But... we don't know the first thing about operating a zoo," said Chase.

"I know, but I guess either we step up to the plate and become very fast learners, or we can say goodbye to that five million."

"What if we do say no? What will happen to the money?"

"According to Sammie, it will go to a local animal welfare organization in the town where Cousin Beatrice lived, along with the care of her three hundred cats."

"Three hundred cats!" said Chase as he rubbed his face. "I thought having four was already too much." When his wife gave him an odd look, he quickly corrected himself. "I mean, not too much, obviously. A handful, let's just put it like that."

"They are a handful," Odelia agreed. "And I can't imagine what it must be like to have three hundred. On the other hand, we can hire people to take care of them. We don't have to do it all by ourselves. With five million, we can probably get the best people money can buy."

"That money will soon be gone," said Chase. "And then where will we be? We'll have to pay for that personnel out of our pocket."

"We could sell tickets to the zoo," Odelia suggested.

"Who wants to pay good money to look at cats when they can see them all around?"

"Yeah, I guess you're right," said Odelia. Then she perked up again. "If our reality show is a success, we'll have plenty of money coming in that way. Just look at the Kardashians, they're pretty well off."

"We're not the Kardashians, babe. I can't imagine people tuning in to see your grandmother throwing a tantrum, your dad diagnosing a patient, or me chasing some drug dealer. Our lives are not exactly glamorous."

"I don't know," said Odelia. "I think we do lead interesting lives. Maybe not glamorous ones, but there's already enough glamour in the world. Maybe people wouldn't mind watching people like them on television for a change. People who don't look like supermodels and live in million-dollar mansions."

"I don't know," said Chase.

"Look, we can discuss all of this tonight at the family meeting. And then at the end, we'll put it to a vote."

"Okay, fine," said Chase, who didn't need this extra headache, to be honest.

"So how are you getting on with the two Fisher murders?"

"Three Fisher murders," he corrected her.

Her eyes went a little wider. "Three?"

He nodded. "I have a hunch Allison Fisher was also murdered. Though we'll have to wait for the post-mortem results to know for sure."

"Imagine that. Three members of the same family murdered."

"Have you found the Fishers' dog yet?"

"No, I haven't. Max and the others have looked all over town, but so far they haven't been able to find her. Which is a pity, since she clearly knows who killed them. Only she refused to tell Max, telling him that she was glad that Chloe was dead, since she had been treating her horribly and deserved to be killed."

"Harsh," Chase grunted.

"Yeah, she must have suffered a great deal at the hands of her humans. And the odd thing is that the Pet Owners Society had received a complaint about the Fishers, which is why Gran had gone there this morning to talk to them. Under the guise of setting up an award for best pet parent, she was going to try and ascertain if there were any grounds for the complaint."

"Obviously there were, if what that dog told your cats is true."

"I think it was. Max said she struck him as a reliable witness."

He thought for a moment. "Okay, so better tell them to

keep looking. So far nobody has come forward as a witness, so we need to find that dog."

Odelia got up. "So you'll think about the inheritance business? And I'll invite my uncle, Charlene, Mom, and Dad for the meeting. We need to decide this as a family because it's probably going to impact us all."

"Nothing probably about it," he said. "This is going to change our lives, babe. For better or for worse, I'm not sure yet."

The moment his wife was gone, he returned to the case he'd been investigating. Officers had gone door to door to interview the Fishers' neighbors, but so far no one had seen anything out of the ordinary, which struck him as very strange, since Mike Fisher had actually run out of his front door, the killer giving chase, had made it as far as the garden house across the street before he was struck down. Someone must have seen it. Of course, it was their luck that the people across the street weren't home, and neither were most of the Fishers' neighbors since most of them had been at work that morning, as was to be expected. But even the people who had been home said they had heard nothing out of the ordinary, hadn't seen any suspicious cars or unknown persons lurking about the neighborhood the last couple of days. And when asked what they thought of the Fishers, all of them had confirmed they were nice people, sociable and well-liked in the neighborhood, though one woman had complained that Mike Fisher liked to leave his trash cans out on the street until the day after trash collection day, something she had thought very inconsiderate.

Inconsiderate, maybe, but surely not bad enough to warrant murder.

He checked the testimony of the woman once again but couldn't find anything that raised any red flags. Retired, eighty-three, lived three houses down from the Fishers. No criminal record and lived alone.

He sat back with a sigh. So two people are murdered in broad daylight, and nobody saw anything? How was that possible? Almost as if they had died by an invisible hand that had struck down from out of nowhere.

And as he closed his eyes for a moment, he found himself hoping that Max would find this missing dog, or else the investigation would be over before it even got started.

Though he still had other arrows in his quiver. He had applied to the phone company for Mike, Chloe, and Allison's phone records. He had applied to the bank for their bank records. And he had delivered their mobile phones and laptops to the tech department so they could take a closer look at their conversations, messages, and emails. Hopefully, one of these leads would yield something. And then, of course, he had arranged to interview the couple's relatives, friends, and Mike's colleagues to dig a little deeper into their personal lives and hopefully form a picture of the kind of family they had been.

Sooner or later, he would hit on something. Something that sparked an idea. Someone who had felt aggrieved or upset with something Mike or Chloe had done. Or maybe there was a family feud they didn't know about. Someone somewhere had a motive for what they did to that family, and he would find it.

CHAPTER 9

When Robert Ross arrived home after walking Marlin, he decided to tell his wife about the strange story he'd heard at the dog park. He found Kimberly in the backyard where she was pruning her beloved gardenias. "I heard the most incredible story, honey," he said after pressing a kiss to the top of her head. "I talked to Kurt Mayfield and Ted Trapper at the dog park, and do you know what they told me?"

"I have absolutely no idea," said his wife as she spread some more mulch on the soil.

"Remember Vesta Muffin, who lives over on Harrington Street?"

"How could I not remember her? We're in the same society, after all."

Even though Kimberly had claimed that Hampton Cove was a social dead zone, she had, after long debate, decided to join the Pet Owners Society. It was an organization that prided itself on safeguarding the health and well-being of pets. To that end, the society had even set up a novel initiative where its members paid visits to pet owners in town under the guise of looking for the best pet owners who could then win an award. But in actual fact, they were there to inspect the living conditions of the pets and see if they were being treated well.

"Okay, so Kurt and Ted claim that Vesta can actually talk to her cats. And not just her, but also her daughter and her granddaughter."

Kimberly frowned. "Now that is absolute and complete nonsense, Robert. They were probably pulling your leg."

"I thought so too, but they seemed adamant. I don't believe them, of course, but wouldn't it be amazing if we could talk to Marlin?"

Kimberly directed a critical look at the big dog of indeterminate pedigree. "Maybe," she allowed. "It certainly would make the work of the society a lot easier if we could simply interview these pets and ask them if they are being treated well or not. Instead of having to use this roundabout way of ascertaining their well-being." She frowned. "Though if Vesta can actually talk to pets, then why doesn't she simply ask these dogs how they're doing?"

"She can talk to cats, not dogs. Kurt and Ted took great pains to point that out. But apparently, their cats can talk to dogs and other species, and they relay their words to their humans." He grinned. "Pretty sure they were pulling my leg, but you should have seen how they tried to keep a straight face!"

"Mm," said Kimberly, but he could see that she wasn't all that interested in his stories. So he decided to go inside for a cooling drink, and while he was at it, check to see if Marlin's water bowl was still full. After the walk they'd had, and the time Marlin had spent gamboling with his friends at the dog park, he was probably dying of thirst. The last thing they needed was for the Pet Owners Society to send one of their emissaries to check on them!

He now took out his phone to scan the news. As a news addict, he didn't just read the national papers, but after having moved to Hampton Cove, he had also gotten into the habit of perusing the *Hampton Cove Gazette*, their local paper mostly written by Odelia Kingsley, the so-called cat talker, if Kurt and Ted were to be believed.

He saw that a couple of new entries had been posted to the *Gazette* site and quickly scanned them. One article in particular drew his attention. A couple had been murdered that morning. Mike and Chloe Fisher, brutally attacked in their home by a person or persons unknown.

He looked up from his phone and wondered where he had heard those names before? And then he got it. According to his wife, the Fishers featured on a list of people who mistreated their pets, and a member of the society had been dispatched to investigate. He remembered how upset Kimberly had been when she first heard about it. She might not be all that crazy about Marlin, but that was more because she wasn't fond of the fact that he didn't have a pedigree. But she did love animals and could get very upset when she heard stories about people not treating them well.

Apparently, someone had decided to teach those pet haters a lesson but had gone too far.

* * *

Kevin Thomson was back in his attic. After setting out the bait, he certainly hoped the Pooles would bite. If they didn't, he'd have to find some other way of proving beyond a shadow of a doubt that they could talk to their cats. But he had a feeling they would accept his terms. Five million was a lot of money, after all. A big carrot to dangle in front of anyone's nose. Most people would jump at the chance to grab the big prize, figuring they'd won the lottery. And to accept a slight loss of privacy was a small price to pay for the privilege of becoming rich.

Though Odelia herself hadn't seemed all that excited about the reality show idea. And when he listened via the bugs he had planted in the house of her mom and dad while he paid a visit to the bathroom, they were organizing a family meeting to discuss the pros and cons of the idea. He hoped they'd say yes. His career depended on it. If he didn't land this story with a resounding bang, he might very possibly have to kiss his career at the *Chronicle* goodbye, and also any future prospects at other, more respectable papers. And so he fervently hoped that Vesta Muffin, as the old lady's name was, could convince the others to accept the bait. She seemed to be more inclined than her granddaughter to move ahead with the plan.

The only problem was where he was going to find three hundred cats? But then he figured he'd deal with that later. First hook the fish, then provide the cats. He shivered slightly as he imagined having to deal with no less than three hundred of those horrible creatures. Even as a kid, he'd hated cats with a vengeance, and he simply couldn't imagine how people could actually live with the little monsters. Just the noise they made was terrifying and cut him right to the bone, like nails dragging across a blackboard. Those Pooles were crazy, that was the only possible explanation. But then soon they'd be exposed to the whole world, and he'd surf on the fame the story would garner to even greater heights. The Pooles might be a family of crazy freaks, but they were going to make him rich. Rich and famous!

CHAPTER 10

The first person we decided to talk to was Suzette Peters, who had arrived at the house when we were there and had introduced herself as Mike Fisher's colleague. An officer had taken her statement, but Chase wanted to have a word with her and see if she couldn't shed some more light on the tragedy.

We found her at home, where she had been sent by her boss after he learned about what had happened at the Fisher home. Clearly, Suzette had been much impressed or perhaps even traumatized to some extent. She opened the door of her roomy apartment and led us inside into the cozy salon, dominated by a large flatscreen television. Little knick-knacks made the place very pleasant to be in, and I liked her sense of style. Immediately, Chase launched into his first question, wanting to know more about her relationship with Mike Fisher.

"Well, he was my supervisor, you know," said the woman. "I've only been with MicMacAdam for three months, you see, and he was the person training me for the job."

"What is it exactly that you do at MicMacAdam, Suzette?" asked Odelia.

"I write copy for ad campaigns. Junior copywriter is my official title, while Mike Fisher was one of the senior copywriters. He was great at what he did. Possibly the best copywriter in the entire agency. The way he could turn a phrase and make it sing was simply... magical." Her eyes had gone wide, and a blush had crept up her cheeks. Here sat a person, I thought, who had a serious crush on Mike Fisher.

"So why did he invite you to come to his house? Was this something he often did with the people he was supervising?"

"I don't think so. It's just that... we were working on a big project for a major client, and we had a presentation coming up next week. So we were pushing to try and be ready before the deadline. But Mike said he needed to be home today for personal reasons, and could I drop by the house so we could work on our presentation some more? So obviously, I said yes, even though it felt a little awkward, you know. I mean, you hear these stories about senior partners in a company hitting on the new hires, but I don't think Mike was that kind of guy. I even asked one of the older colleagues, and she said she'd never heard even a whisper about that sort of thing, though she did advise me not to say yes next time and maybe talk to Mike's partner Bruno McIntyre, who's one of the other co-founders of MicMacAdam, if I felt any qualms, which I must admit I did." She was wringing her hands, and I wondered if Mike was the kind of guy who hit on his junior staff. It was entirely possible, of course. Then again, his wife had been home, so he wasn't going to do that sort of thing when she was there, surely?

Suzette stared at the floor for a moment before continuing. Her cheeks had acquired the same color as her hair, which I would have called bright auburn. She was a very attractive young woman, and I could understand her qualms.

Being invited to your direct superior's home for some nebulous reason would cause all sorts of alarm bells to go off in anyone's head.

"The thing you have to know about Mike is that he was completely unaware of how good he really was. Other agencies had been trying to steal him away from MicMacAdam, but he simply ignored them. Headhunters had been calling him, offering him large sums of money, but he said he wasn't interested in the money, he simply loved the work. And also, he and his college friends Bruno McIntyre and Adam Kaur founded the company together, so he wouldn't dream of leaving the agency in the lurch by signing with one of the big players."

"Are you sure about that?" asked Chase. "That Mike wasn't planning to leave? If they dangled a big enough bag of money in front of his nose, he might have decided to take the offer, loyalty to his college buddies or not."

But Suzette shook her head decidedly. "Like I said, Mike wasn't like that. Money didn't mean anything to him, or fame, or even success. He loved the work and he put his heart and soul into it, you know? I mean, just being in the same room with the man, to watch him work—it was sheer genius, and so, so inspiring." She straightened and gave us a vague smile. "Mike Fisher was a genius, and his loss will be badly felt throughout not just MicMacAdam but the entire industry. We have lost one of our greats today. Maybe the greatest."

"Okay, so you arrived at... ten o'clock?" asked Chase, consulting his notebook.

"Yeah, the meeting was at ten, so I wanted to arrive right on time. Only when I got there, nobody answered the door, so I went around the back and ran into this old lady who told me that there had been an incident." She put a hand to her mouth and her eyes welled up. "Mike's wife was dead. And then later, it transpired that Mike himself had also been killed."

"And Mike and Chloe's daughter, Allison," Odelia added.

"Oh, my god!" said Suzette. "The whole family? Dead?"

Odelia nodded sadly. "Did you know the Fishers? Apart from Mike, I mean."

"No, I didn't. Mike talked about Chloe and Allison, of course, and I'd seen a picture on his desk of Mike with his wife and daughter. But I'd never met them or knew much about them, except for what people at the office had told me."

"And what did they tell you?"

Suzette hesitated, then when Odelia gave her an encouraging smile, forged ahead. "That Chloe Fisher was a... how do I say this politely? Well, let's just say she was not a nice person."

"In what sense?" asked Chase.

"In the sense that she was a bully and that she was mean to Mike."

"And to their dog," Dooley added quietly.

"How was she mean? You mean she got physical with her husband?"

"No, more like emotionally, you know, and verbally. Calling him names. He could never do anything right. She was always on his case, criticizing him and being angry with him."

"How do people know all this? Did Chloe come into the office sometimes?"

"They saw her at office parties, and when she had too much to drink, she would lose all sense of self-restraint and really start laying into him. Calling him... well, some very bad names, actually. She had a very extensive vocabulary."

"But you never personally witnessed this," said Chase.

"No, like I said I've only been with the company for three

months, but colleagues have told me. Apparently, the last office party was the worst. They actually had to restrain Chloe and put her in a cab home after she had laid into her husband for not topping up her drink fast enough and for spending too much time talking to a colleague. There was talk of divorce, but when Mike was back at the office on Monday, he acted as if nothing happened. And when people asked him about it, he brushed it off. He said his wife hadn't felt well, and they shouldn't blame her for what happened. He also said she was taking pills, and they didn't mix well with alcohol. He was called into the office of his partner, though nobody knows what was discussed behind closed doors, and of course, Bruno didn't say."

"So Bruno McIntyre is the CEO?"

She nodded.

"What position did Mike have?"

"He was the Chief Creative Officer. The CCO."

"And this... Adam Kaur?"

"He died a couple of years ago. He was in charge of the financial side of things."

"One more question, Suzette," said Chase. "Where were you this morning before you arrived at the Fishers'?"

"At the office. I wanted to put in some work before my meeting with Mike. And then I took an Uber at... nine-thirty, I guess?"

"Can anyone verify that?"

"My colleagues and the Uber driver, of course."

Odelia and Chase thanked Suzette for her time, and we left.

"Suzette's story confirms what Bella told us, Max," said Dooley once we were back in the car. "She also said that Chloe was a witch and that she used to pinch her and call her names."

"Yeah, she also used to pinch Mike," I said. "Though I can't imagine a grown man accepting that kind of abuse from his wife."

"But the office party, Max! She was very mean at the office party!"

"Yeah, that was the moment the cat got out of the bag," I said.

He stared at me. "What cat? When did it get out of the bag?"

"Just an expression," I assured him. "Chloe showed her true colors under the influence of too much alcohol and showed all of Mike's colleagues what kind of person she really was."

"So is it possible that Mike killed his wife and then he killed himself?"

"Doubtful," I said. "The sequence of events doesn't seem to bear that out."

"Or maybe Chloe killed her husband and then killed herself?"

"But then who killed Allison Fisher?" I asked. "She also died, remember?"

"Oh, this is so complicated, Max!" he cried.

It was complicated because we weren't in possession of all the facts pertaining to the case yet. Once we were, it would probably become clear what exactly happened that morning.

"Finally," said Chase as he checked his phone. He turned to his wife. "Coroner's preliminary report on Allison Fisher. I asked Abe to fast-track it." He frowned as he read from the report. "Looks like she died from drowning, after all," he said. "No signs of any other injuries. She had water in her lungs, the kind of water consistent with the lake, and time of death would have been around midnight last night." His frown deepened. "That doesn't make sense. So she drowned last night, and then this morning both her parents are murdered?"

"Maybe the two aren't connected?" Odelia suggested. "It is perfectly possible that the Fishers didn't even know that their daughter had drowned. How old was she?"

"Seventeen."

"So she probably stayed out late often. So last night wouldn't have been an exception. She was out late, maybe went to a party, then got into the lake and drowned. Did she have alcohol in her system, or any illegal substances?"

Chase returned to the report. "Nothing. No alcohol, no nothing. Toxicology report is clean. So why did she drown? And where was she last night?"

"That's for us to find out," said Odelia, sounding a lot more chipper than Chase looked.

And since there is no time like the present, they decided to pay a visit to Mike's partner first and then try to figure out how Allison Fisher had ended up in that lake.

CHAPTER 11

Bruno McIntyre, as Suzette had already indicated, was the big boss at MicMacAdam. He was a handsome man with an athletic physique, tanned face, and a stylishly coiffed but suspiciously dark beard in lieu of the hair that used to be on top of his head but was now gone. He seemed genuinely undone by what had happened to his friend and partner.

"I can't believe Mike is gone," he said. "He was such a powerhouse, you know. This entire company ran on the energy that he generated. Without him, I don't know what we will do."

"He was the Chief Creative Officer?"

"Yeah, he was in charge of the creative side of the company, while I'm more the money guy and also trying to land new accounts, of course. But the real genius of MicMacAdam and the reason we are where we are today was Mike. And I knew it from the very beginning. When we met in college he was already the guy he still was today, his mind always buzzing with ideas. He had this creative energy that made it very appealing to be around him. He liked to think out loud, and the stuff that sometimes came out of his mouth was simply..." He put two fingers to his lips and kissed them. "Pure brilliance. And he wasn't just a creative powerhouse but also a pleasure to work with. Inspiring. Plenty of people who work here now applied for a job at MicMacAdam just so they could learn from Mike. The guy was a legend in our industry, and he will be sorely missed."

"Okay, so we talked to one of his colleagues, and she told us a story about Mike and his wife Chloe not getting along all that well," asked Chase. "What can you tell us about that?"

The man's face clouded. He had one of those faces that was a limpid pool of emotion. Anything that went through his mind, you could see reflected on his face. "Yeah, that was bad," he said. "Those two fought like cats and dogs, though it's probably more accurate to say that Chloe fought and Mike took it on the chin."

"He never fought back?"

"Never. He was too much of a gentleman for that. Never hit a woman and all that, you know."

"So their fights sometimes got physical?"

"Well..."

"Mr. McIntyre, did Chloe Fisher hit her husband?"

He bowed his head. "Yes, she did. Once Mike arrived at work with a black eye, and immediately I knew what must have happened. He blamed it on the pills Chloe was taking. She had trouble regulating her moods. She was seeing a shrink but also taking pills. And sometimes the mix wasn't right, and she could get completely unbalanced, and then she took it out on him. He didn't blame her. He said she was a sick person and she couldn't help it. All he wanted was for her to get the help she needed. But that was easier said than done, apparently."

"Did it affect his work? Or the company?" asked Odelia.

"It didn't affect his work, I don't think. And he never talked about it, certainly not to his clients."

"So MicMacAdam wasn't negatively impacted by their fights?"

The CEO and founder stared at Odelia, then smiled. "I see what you're doing here, Mrs. Kingsley. You're trying to construct a motive for why I would have harmed Chloe or Mike or both. But I can tell you right now that doesn't make any sense. First off, Mike left his personal stuff at home where it belonged, except that one time at the office party, but he promised me that would never happen again. And secondly," he added, spreading his arms, "I loved the guy. He wasn't just my colleague and co-founder but also my very good friend. We took vacations together with our families, we celebrated birthdays, Christmas, you name it. Last year we even climbed Mount Kilimanjaro together, just him and me. We left the wives at home for the occasion. And we had a great time. Bonding, you know, like the best friends that we were. So no, I would never kill Mike Fisher if that's what you're trying to imply."

"And Chloe Fisher?"

"Never! Of course not. I'm not a killer. I couldn't do it. Murder a person in cold blood? Impossible. I can't even kill a mosquito. I hate the sight of blood. Ask anyone. Ask my wife. I'm the most peaceable person on the planet. A real softie."

"But a shark in business," said Odelia with a smile.

"Well, you have to be, otherwise you'll be out of business pretty quickly."

"So what about Allison Fisher?" asked Chase.

"Allison? What about her?"

"How was the relationship between Allison and her parents?"

"Good, I would say, though the last couple of years it had deteriorated somewhat. Especially the relationship between

Allison and her mom had become seriously strained. Last time I saw Allison, she even told me that she couldn't wait to go off to college so she could get away from her mom, who was really getting on her nerves. But then, it can't have been easy to live in that house, with all the tension that seemed to be so prevalent all the time. But Allison was handling it well, I thought. She was very mature for her age."

"You wouldn't know where she was last night, would you?"

"No, I wouldn't. I know the family well, but not well enough that I would know what Allison was up to on a week night. Though if I had to venture a guess, I'd say she was probably with her boyfriend."

"Name?" asked Chase.

"Um..." Bruno frowned and closed his eyes for a moment. "Liam... Cass? Yeah. Liam Cass. He's in her class, and they've been together for a while now. Though with Allison going off to college soon, I think it's safe to say they were having some trouble."

"Liam isn't going to the same college?"

"Liam isn't going to college, period."

"And why is that?"

"Because his dad is Carroll Cass." When Odelia and Chase stared at him, he smiled. "Cass Motors? He runs the biggest Ford dealership in town, and Liam has been working for him since he turned fourteen. There's absolutely no way Carroll would send his kid off to college. Liam is going to take over the dealership when his old man retires, and that decision was made a long time ago and is pretty much set in stone."

"So the couple was about to be split up?"

Bruno nodded. "And Liam wasn't happy about it. Not happy at all."

CHAPTER 12

We found Allison's boyfriend at Cass Motors, where he worked as a mechanic. Liam Cass hadn't been told yet that his girlfriend had died, and so that difficult task was upon Chase. After he had broken the news to the kid, Liam broke down and used an oily rag to wipe at his tears, causing his already-smushed face to become even more smushed than it was before.

"I can't believe this," he said, sobbing incoherently. "Allison is dead? But how?"

"She drowned in Lake Mario," said Chase as he placed a hand on the young man's shoulder. "I'm sorry, Liam. I'm very sorry."

We were standing next to what is commonly termed a grease pit, where cars are repaired by the mechanics working in the garage. It wasn't as shiny and clean as in the showroom, and it was actually funny to see the big contrast. But out here, the work that was done was more than appreciated by the car owners whose cars had broken down and had to be repaired. And obviously, Liam was good at what he did, despite his young age, for he had been given his own pit, where he worked solo on the cars that had been entrusted to him.

"Did you see Allison last night?" asked Chase.

Liam nodded. "Yeah, we met at her place, then went out driving."

"Where did you go?"

"Oh, here and there," he said vaguely. "She just liked to get away, you know. She couldn't be under the same roof with that woman."

"Her mother?"

"Yeah. She was just the worst. Always screaming and acting hysterical. Allie just couldn't take it anymore. She said she needed to get out of there before something really terrible happened." He looked up. "She wasn't... you know... murdered or anything, was she?"

"We're not sure yet," Chase said.

"It's just that, with that mother of hers, you could expect anything. She was crazy, that one. When she saw my face, she already started screaming and shouting. Figuring I wasn't good enough for her precious daughter, and telling me to stop harassing them."

"So you went for a drive? And then what happened?" asked Chase.

"Well, we just drove around for a while, then stopped by the ocean and ate the stuff I'd picked up at the drive-through. Allison just loved Happy Meals. Had since she was a kid. Back when her mom wasn't crazy yet, or so she said. So she kept the habit, and every time we went for a drive, I had to pick her up a Happy Meal. It made her happy," he added with a shrug. "So we ate as we watched the ocean and talked about life, you know, and the future."

"If Allison went off to college, you weren't going to see much of her anymore."

He hung his head and wiped at his nose. "Yeah, that was a

bit of a problem for me. I had this idea that she was going to drop me like a rock, you know? The moment she left? She said that wasn't going to happen and that she loved me, but I don't know. Once she got involved with those college kids, she would forget all about me. And so we argued about that a lot. She said I had to trust her, and I tried to, but it was hard. And then her mom kept telling me it was over, and they were finally getting rid of me. Looked to me as if Allie was getting rid of all of us. All of Hampton Cove and all of her past. She was leaving and didn't plan to come back, whatever she said."

"What makes you say that?"

He showed us a pendant that hung around his neck. It sported a dolphin. "She gave me this last night. Said it was to celebrate the fact we'd been together one year. But to me, it felt as if it was her going-away present. Or a goodbye-I'll-be-seeing-you-around-maybe present."

"So after you finished your Happy Meal and watched the ocean, then what?" asked Chase.

"We drove back into town, and she asked me to drop her off at her friend's house. Said she had some stuff to take care of."

"What stuff?"

"Homework."

"Okay, so what friend was this?"

"Melissa Bell. She and Allison had been friends since kindergarten. Joined at the hip, those two."

"He sounds jealous, Max," said Dooley.

"Maybe he was," I agreed.

"What time was this?" asked Chase.

"Around... nine, nine-thirty maybe? I didn't look at the clock."

"So you dropped her off at Melissa Bell's place, and then?"

"Then I went home."

"Can anyone verify that?"

He frowned at the cop. "Why? Why are you asking me all these questions?"

"Just routine, Liam," Odelia assured him. "We're asking everyone these questions."

"Well, I saw my mom, I guess, when I walked in the door. She was watching something on TV. She asked if I wanted to join her, but I wasn't in the mood, so I went upstairs to my room. I spent half an hour on my phone, and then I fell asleep. I've been combining my studies with my job at the garage, you know, and by the time my head hits the pillow, I'm out like a light."

"Why weren't you in the mood to watch television with your mom?"

"Because I just wasn't, all right?" he said, getting a little worked up.

"All right, all right," said Chase. "No need to get upset, Liam."

"If you keep asking me these questions, I'm bound to get upset, aren't I? You make me feel like you're suspecting me of something. But I swear that the last time I saw Allison, she was alive. And besides, I thought you said she drowned?"

"She did drown, but it's not so easy to determine whether a person drowned because they slipped and fell in or because someone pushed them in and held their head under water."

He stared at the cop. "So you are saying she *was* murdered?"

"I'm saying that we don't know what happened, but we're determined to find out."

"I can't believe this," he said. "Murdered." Then his expression hardened. "Must be that mother of hers. She hated Allison. You should have heard the kinds of things she said to her. Vile, vicious things. Stuff no normal person would say to their daughter."

"You think Chloe could have harmed her own daughter?" asked Odelia.

"Oh, absolutely. That woman was out of her mind. She was capable of anything. Though why she would be meeting Allie in the middle of the night at Lake Mario is beyond me."

"Have you ever met her up there?"

"Never. Allison preferred the ocean. Lakes gave her the creeps. She always said she thought strange creatures lived at the bottom of that lake, and if she went in, they would grab her by the ankle and drag her down."

"So you didn't meet her by the lake last night?"

"No, I didn't. Like I said, she had plans, and those plans obviously didn't include me."

I had the impression he wasn't merely referring to doing homework with Allison's friend Melissa Bell.

CHAPTER 13

We met Liam's dad in the office. Contrary to his son, who wore greased-up coveralls, Carroll Cass was dressed to the nines in a snazzy suit that suited him well. He resembled his son but had gained a few pounds over the years. Like Mr. McIntyre he also sported an intricate facial hair arrangement that must take up a significant amount of time to groom each morning. Nevertheless, it suited him and concealed his jowly cheeks.

"Tragic," he announced upon learning of the deaths of Allison, Mike, and Chloe Fisher. "I loved Allie like a daughter and thought she made a fine addition to the family. How did she drown?"

"We're not sure yet," Chase said. "Can you confirm where your son was at midnight last night, sir?"

The garage owner frowned. "Um... well, to be honest, I have no idea. I mean, I suppose he was in his room, but I didn't check if that's what you want to know. Liam is a big boy, and even though he still lives at home, I respect his privacy, and he respects ours. So, no, I couldn't tell you where he was at midnight."

"He says he walked by his mom watching television when he arrived home around nine-thirty and then went upstairs to his room. So, where were you, sir?"

"Well, I was sitting right next to my wife, watching that same television," said Carroll with a disarming smile. "The wife loves this *Masked Singer* nonsense, and even though I keep swearing I won't watch it, I still get roped in every time."

"Liam didn't mention you."

"What can I tell you? That boy probably had other things on his mind."

"Like what?"

"He was in a funk lately. His girlfriend was going off to college, and he had this fixed idea that she was breaking up with him, even though everyone could see how good those two were together and how much Allie loved my son. But he was determined to think the worst of the situation, and there was nothing we or anyone else could say to him to change that."

"So you didn't think Allison was breaking up with him by going off to college, sir?" asked Odelia.

"Look, who knows what was going on in that head of hers, right? I mean, she was seventeen, for crying out loud. When I was seventeen, half the time I didn't know which way my head was pointing. So I think she probably had no idea herself what was going to happen. The main reason she was so eager to go off to college was to get away from the frankly toxic atmosphere that was prevalent at her home, with her mom and dad fighting like cats and dogs. She wasn't thinking about Liam or their relationship. And once she was off, let the chips fall where they may, you know."

"Even if they fell in such a way that Liam would lose his girlfriend?"

He shrugged. "Such is life, I guess. He would have gotten

over it if she was actually breaking up with him, which, as I said, I don't think she planned to do. But now I guess we'll never know."

"If Liam and Allison got married, your son would have become a part of this 'toxic' environment you mentioned," said Chase. "That mustn't have sat well with you."

"No, it sure as heck didn't," said the garage owner, drumming his fingers on his desk. "Where are you going with this? Are you saying that I killed the Fishers? Because I can tell you right now that you're barking up the wrong tree here. Okay, so I wasn't fond of that couple—well, maybe Mike, but definitely not Chloe, who probably had some undiagnosed mental illness. But that doesn't mean I would have gone out there and killed them. If I wanted to protect my boy from the Fishers, I would have simply advised him to stay away. Allison was doing the same thing. She told everyone who would listen that the moment she turned eighteen, she was leaving and she was never coming back."

"Leaving Hampton Cove for good?"

"Leaving her parents' home. She hated the way those two treated each other and couldn't get out of that house fast enough so she could stand on her own two feet. And I was all for it. I had even offered her a job here at Cass Motors so she and Liam could get married and move in together."

"And did she accept your kind offer, sir?"

He looked away. "Nah. She was fixated on this college thing. Thought it was going to be the start of a whole new life. Had all these illusions that a college education was going to solve all of her problems. I could have told her that she was harboring a lot of illusions that simply wouldn't pan out, no matter how hard she studied. A degree is all nice and good, but it's not the panacea that a lot of these kids seem to think it is. Hell, look at me. I never got a college degree, and I made something of myself. Just opened a third garage in

Hampton Keys with plans to open a fourth. But I knew she would warm to the idea eventually, once she saw that sticking your nose in books isn't the answer to life's problems." He smiled. "But then we've all been young, haven't we? We've all had these illusions that life has cured us from."

"One final question, sir," said Chase.

"Shoot," the motor mogul said magnanimously.

"Where were you this morning at ten o'clock?"

"This morning? Um, let me think. Well, right here in my office. I had a meeting with the other dealership managers about a new campaign we're launching. A thousand bucks cashback for the new model, and zero percent financing for thirty-six months. How about that for a stunt, huh? And we're throwing in a couple of accessories for the early deciders as well. You can't go wrong with Cass Motors! So how about it? Wanna see the latest beauty in our line-up? But I'm warning you. The moment you take a seat in this baby, you'll never want to get out again. You won't be able to leave this showroom without taking her for a spin."

Chase and Odelia politely declined, much to the car dealership owner's disappointment. But I had a feeling he'd get over it soon.

CHAPTER 14

The next person on our list was Mr. Cass's wife and Liam's mother. Stella Cass was a handsome woman in her late forties with abundantly curly red hair and a trim figure she probably worked hard to maintain. Like her husband and son, she, too, worked at Cass Motors. In her case, she worked the reception desk where she greeted the customers walking into the dealership and also handled requests from those unfortunate souls whose cars had broken down and needed to be repaired.

She combined a no-nonsense attitude with a lot of charm and genuine warmth, and I liked her immediately. Unlike her husband, there was nothing artificial about her, except maybe the color of her hair.

"Yeah, I heard what happened from Liam just now," she announced when we talked to her in the little meeting room where her husband's salespersons met potential customers and tried to dazzle them with deals and possibilities. All around us hung posters of Ford motor cars, and the place smelled of new cars. On the table, plenty of glossy brochures lay extolling the virtues of those same cars. "It's really sad, especially about Allie, of course, who was just the sweetest girl possible. Not a bad bone in her body, that one. Which always surprised me, considering she came from those people," she said with an expression of contempt.

"You didn't like Allison's parents?" asked Odelia.

"Nobody liked Allie's parents, especially her mom, who had a knack for putting people off. We had dinner together once, you know, not long after Allie and Liam announced that they'd been seeing each other for a while. We figured we should get to know her parents, seeing as they might become our in-laws at some point."

"So how did that go?"

"It was an unmitigated disaster. At first, they were polite and everything was fine, but then Chloe started drinking, and the more alcohol entered her bloodstream, the nastier she became. First with jabs against her husband, who just sat there like a sad sack taking one hit after another without retaliating, then she started taking potshots at us, claiming Ford cars have the worst track record of all cars on the market, and weren't we ashamed to be selling that junk. And then when that didn't manage to get a rise out of us, she moved on to Liam, who she accused of selling himself short and taking the easy way out by working at the dealership instead of going off to college like Allie. She claimed Liam had so much going for him and he could really make something of himself if he got the chance. She basically accused us of holding our son back for our own benefit." The corners of her lips had gone down as she remembered that night. "Suffice it to say, we never had another dinner together. The woman was simply vile, detective. Absolutely vile."

"So how did your husband react, or Liam?" asked Odelia.

"They were smart enough not to allow themselves to be provoked. But on the way home, Liam did say that maybe Chloe had a point, and that maybe he had taken the easy way out. He said maybe he should join Allie when she left for college, and it wasn't too late yet."

"And how did you feel about that?"

"Well, we weren't happy, of course. But if he really wanted to go to college, we weren't going to stop him. It was his choice to work at the garage. Even when he was a kid, all he wanted was to work with the other mechanics, and he couldn't wait until he turned fourteen so he could start helping out around the place. And he's good. He's got a real aptitude for the work. And what's more, he loves it—genuinely loves tinkering with engines and taking them apart to find out what's wrong. It's good, honest work, and Chloe was wrong to look down her nose at what we do here at Cass Motors. And if she had managed to turn Liam's head and make him forget what he loves to do, that would have been on her, because it wouldn't have made him happy. It would have made him frustrated. But lucky for him, he finally got that."

"He didn't want to go to college?"

Stella shook her head. "He talked to a couple of people who had gone to NYU, the college Allie had chosen, and I don't know what they told him, but he soon wised up and even told me how lucky he was to have found what it was he wanted to do with his life so soon instead of wasting years like some of these people." She smiled. "I can't tell you how happy that made me, you know."

"So there are a few practical things we need to clear up," said Chase, as he consulted his notebook. "First, there's Liam's statement that he arrived home around nine-thirty last night and saw you in the living room watching television. He then went up to his room and said he decided to sleep early since he was beat. Can you confirm your son's statement, Stella?"

"Absolutely. The *Masked Singer* was on when he came

walking in, and it was a double-length episode, so even though I'm not sure about the time, it must have been around nine-thirty, as he says."

"And did you check on him later, to make sure he was still in his room?"

"No, I didn't," she said ruefully. "Why, do you think he had something to do with what happened to Allie? Because I can tell you right now he wouldn't have harmed a hair on that girl's head. He adored her, you know. Those two were so crazy about each other."

"But he was worried that she would break up with him."

"Yeah, he was, the poor boy. I could have told him he was making a big fuss over nothing. I actually asked Allie about it —we were very close, Allie and me, she even told me once she considered me her real mother, not the monster she was forced to live with at home—and she said she loved Liam and knew in her heart that he was the one for her and they'd be together always. But that she had to pursue her dream of going to college, even if it meant it might put a strain on their relationship. But she also knew that if their bond was strong, they would survive as a couple."

"She considered it like a test."

"Exactly. A relationship test. But she had every confidence they'd succeed."

"Even though Liam didn't share that view."

"No, but then Liam often felt insecure around Allie, especially now that she was going to get a college education and would become a college graduate at some point, maybe get a fancy degree and move up in the world while he would always be nothing but a grease monkey, as he called it. But even though I told him that he was just as valuable as a person as any college graduate, he still found it hard to wrap his head around the fact that Allie was going away and becoming a different person." She shrugged. "She wasn't going to change. She was always going to be Allie, no matter how many degrees she got, you know."

"So about your husband," said Chase.

"What about him?"

"Was he also watching the *Masked Singer* with you last night?"

Stella hesitated for a moment, her eyes flitting to the showroom, then back to her present company. She finally nodded. "Absolutely. He keeps saying he hates it, but he can't miss a single episode. Deep down, he's a big softie, my Carroll is."

"And what about this morning?" asked Odelia. "Let's say at ten o'clock?"

"Oh, I was right here at Cass Motors. And so," she said when Odelia opened her mouth to ask a follow-up question, "were my husband and my son. We may not have liked Allie's parents, but that doesn't mean we were going to kill them." She laughed. "If I were to murder every single person I didn't like, the world would be a slaughterhouse." She realized how that sounded and quickly added, "I mean, we all got people we don't like, right? But we don't go around murdering them. At least I don't."

CHAPTER 15

Melissa Bell may have been Allison's best friend, but when we went in search of her at their school, she didn't seem exactly overwhelmed with grief. We found her laughing and clearly enjoying herself with a young man her own age in the school playground. According to the principal Odelia and Chase had spoken to and had asked permission to speak with Melissa, they had assembled all of their students in the school gym that morning to announce the sad news of Allison's tragic death. They had then offered the assistance of the school counselors for any students who felt overwhelmed with grief by the news. Those students who wished to go home had been given permission to do so, and part of the regular schedule had been canceled.

But Melissa didn't seem to suffer any adverse consequences from the death of her best friend. Though when we approached her and Chase and Odelia showed their badges, she did seem taken aback. "Why do you want to talk to me?" she asked with a touch of defiance. "Shouldn't you ask permission from my parents first? And have an adult present in the room?"

"If you would like, we could arrange all of that," said Chase easily. "Or you could help us clear up some things and get this over with now."

Melissa thought about it for a moment, then finally consented. "What do you want to know?"

"We talked to Liam Cass and he told us that he dropped Allison off at your home last night around nine or nine-thirty. He said you had homework to finish?"

Melissa nodded. "That's right. We met at nine. Allie and I often did our homework together. We'd been doing it since first grade. For some reason it worked better that way."

"So she arrived at nine, and then when did she leave again?"

Melissa hesitated. "Um... I'm not sure. It wasn't that late because my parents don't like it when I stay up too late. And I know that Allie's parents didn't like her staying out late either. So it must have been ten or ten-thirty, maybe? Something like that."

"And did she walk home?"

Melissa nodded. "We didn't live that far apart. So usually she would walk home, and if it got too late, my dad would drive her."

"But last night he didn't?"

"No, she walked. She said she could use some fresh air."

"And why is that, you think?" asked Odelia.

Melissa studied our humans for a moment before responding. "I'm sure you know about this if you talked to Liam, but Allie was thinking about breaking up with him."

"Breaking up with Liam?"

She nodded. "Yeah, she was leaving for college, and frankly, she couldn't wait to get out of here. Away from her parents, away from Hampton Cove, but especially away from Liam."

"But... I thought they were so much in love?"

Melissa laughed a curt laugh. "Yeah, right. Who told you that? Liam? Of course he would say that."

"His mom and dad said the same thing."

"Of course. They knew Allie was a great catch for their precious boy, and they would have done anything to hang on to her and to create the illusion that those two were getting married and moving in together the moment she got back from college. But that wasn't happening. Allie told me that she was sick and tired of Liam chasing after her all the time, following her around like a lovesick puppy, checking her texts every chance he got, and generally acting like a stalker. Did you know that he even followed her around town when he thought she was meeting other boys?"

"And was she? Meeting other boys?"

Melissa made an annoyed gesture. "It wasn't like that. She wasn't interested in that kind of thing, but Liam obviously thought she was. He was insanely jealous and couldn't handle the fact that soon she would be leaving, and then he wouldn't be able to control her anymore."

"But she and Liam drove down to the ocean last night, and they ate a Happy Meal," said Chase, consulting his notes from the interview with Liam.

Melissa rolled her eyes. "The famous Happy Meals. Liam still acted as if Allie was ten years old, but she wasn't. She had outgrown him, and he couldn't see it. Or accept it. So she indulged him, figuring it was only for another couple of weeks, tops, and she didn't need the aggravation."

"Weeks? I thought she wasn't leaving for college until after the summer?"

"She was leaving early. We had arranged everything. I have an aunt who lives in Austin, Texas, and Allie was going to stay with her over the summer, to get familiar with the area."

"She was going to study in Texas?" asked Chase, very much surprised. "But I thought she was going to NYU?"

"That's what she told everybody, especially Liam and also her parents. But in actual fact, she got accepted at the University of Texas and was moving there so she could be as far away from home as possible. And she was never coming back."

Chase and Odelia shared a look of surprise. "This is the first we're hearing of this," said Chase. "Are you sure?"

"Absolutely. Though I was probably one of the only people who knew about this. It wasn't easy, but she had managed to keep it a secret from her parents by faking acceptance papers from NYU, with the real acceptance papers for Texas being sent to my address."

"Did your parents know?"

"They did, yeah."

"And they approved?"

"They knew what Allie's parents were like, especially her mom, and they had agreed a long time ago that they would do anything in their power to help her deal with that mess. So when Allie said she wanted to get as far away from here as she possibly could, we all worked together to make it happen."

"And to hoodwink Allison's family."

Melissa shrugged. "It was the only way. Her mom and dad would never have allowed her to move to Texas on her own. And neither would Liam. In fact, Allison often said that Liam would never let her leave, period. That guy was so crazy about her it bordered on an obsession." Her face clouded. "Once Allie said she had the impression that Liam would rather see her dead than with someone else." She now directed a look of concern at us. "You don't think... She drowned, right? The principal told us this morning that it was an accident?"

"The truth is that we don't know for sure what happened," said Odelia. "Allison drowned, but whether she accidentally stumbled into the water or was pushed is impossible to know without any witnesses."

"Do you have any idea what she was doing out by the lake in the middle of the night, Melissa?" asked Chase. "You said she left around ten o'clock."

"Something like that."

"So how did she end up by the lake at midnight?"

Melissa frowned as she thought about that. "I don't know," she finally admitted. "She said she was going home, and as usual, she didn't want to go, figuring there would be more of the usual drama. So maybe there was more drama, just as she expected, and she ended up leaving the house again because she was so fed up and ended up walking until she found herself by the lake?"

"Is it true that Allison hated the lake? That she was scared of the monsters that lived in the deep?"

She stared at us. "Who told you that?"

"Liam."

Melissa barked incredulously. "That's a lot of nonsense. Allie and I used to hang out by the lake all the time. We even went camping there with our troop when we were little. She never said anything about being scared. On the contrary, she loved swimming and could stay in the water for hours."

"Did she send you any messages last night?"

Melissa shook her head.

"How would you describe her mood?"

"Do you mean, was she suicidal? No, she wasn't. More like fed up, you know. But she couldn't wait to leave for Texas. In fact, it was all she could talk about. I'm also going there, and I'm also excited, but for her, it was as if it was a life and death thing. As if staying here meant she wouldn't live." Her face sagged. "And now, of course, it turns out she was right."

"I'm sorry for saying this, Melissa," said Odelia. "But you don't seem very upset about what happened to your friend."

Melissa gave us a sheepish smile. "We were friends, but we weren't best friends. I mean, I have a lot of friends and Allie was one of them."

"But Liam told us that you were her best friend."

"You know how it is, Mrs. Kingsley: Allie may have considered me her best friend, but that doesn't mean I considered her mine. I liked her, for sure, and my family had done a lot for her, but to be absolutely honest with you..." She hesitated. "Okay, so this is going to sound mean, but I was also fed up with the whole situation, but mostly with Allie always complaining about everything. This stuff with her mom and with Liam was all she ever talked about, you know. It was always me, me, me with her. Her problems, her issues. And sometimes I just wished she would talk about something else for a change. About normal stuff, you know. She was just... too much sometimes."

CHAPTER 16

After our interviews were over, we found ourselves in Uncle Alec's office for a meeting with the Chief about the state of the investigation. Odelia and Chase sat on one side of the big man's desk, with Odelia's uncle on the other side reading through some of the statements Chase had already typed up, as well as the coroner's reports that had come in on the different members of the Fisher family.

"Okay, so it's just as we thought," he said. "Chloe Fisher was killed where she was found, the body not moved. The knife was one of a set of knives in the kitchen."

"So she was murdered with her own kitchen knife?" asked Odelia.

"Yes, that's right. And so was the husband. Though he seems to have made a run for it, but eventually the killer caught up with him and finished him off with the garden shears."

"So... he was stabbed with a kitchen knife and then also with those garden shears?"

Uncle Alec nodded. "Looks like the killer nabbed him in the front room of the house, stabbing him in the stomach, but then Mike escaped through the front door, ran across the street, and got as far as the garden house of his neighbors. Possibly he wanted to hide there. We found droplets of blood on the front doorstep of the neighbor's house, so we think he knocked on the door and rang the bell. But since the Garcias weren't home, that wasn't going to do him a lot of good. At which point he must have realized that the killer was coming after him, and so he tried to hide in the garden house, where he was caught and where a struggle ensued, causing the racks to become unattached from the walls and the tools scattered across the floor. The killer then grabbed the garden shears and stabbed Mike in the chest, this time inflicting a fatal wound."

"But... why didn't the killer use the same knife he stabbed him with earlier?" asked Chase. "That doesn't seem to make a lot of sense."

Uncle Alec shrugged. "I guess he changed his mind. Or maybe he dropped the knife."

"That second knife wasn't found, correct?"

"There was no second knife. That knife was also used to stab Chloe Fisher, only in her case, the killer had better luck and killed her on the first attempt. We found Mike's blood in Chloe's knife wound, which tells us that she was killed after Mike was stabbed."

"Odd that she wouldn't have heard her husband scream for help and try to get away herself," said Odelia. She closed her eyes. "So let's picture the scene. The killer arrives, somehow gains access to the house."

"The door wasn't forced open, so Mike must have let him in," said her uncle.

"Okay, so the killer arrives, and Mike lets him into the house. At some point, the killer must have been in the kitchen, where he took a knife from the block of knives on the countertop and proceeded to stab Mike in the stomach.

This was in the front room. Mike escaped through the front door, and the killer gave chase and ended up killing Mike in his neighbor's garden shed. The killer then returned to the house, with the knife, and stabbed Chloe, who was found at the bottom of the garden, next to the pergola."

"That seems to be the gist of it," said her uncle. "Unless the killer stabbed Mike, who escaped, then the killer went looking for Chloe first, and stabbed her. At which point he went in search of Mike and found him in that garden house."

"And nobody saw or heard anything?"

"Except for the dog," said Uncle Alec, giving me a penetrating look. "The dog who refuses to testify because she hated her humans so much she's having a party to celebrate the fact that they're dead." He shook his head. "I didn't think dogs had it in them. What about 'loyal til I die?' Chloe Fisher must have been a real piece of work if even her own dog hated her so much she's happy that she's dead and she's decided to protect her killer."

"We still haven't found Bella," I said quietly. Though it was also true that we hadn't really looked after our first attempt to track her down. "Maybe we should give it another shot?"

Odelia patted my head. "That would be great, Max. We need her testimony."

"It's odd that none of the neighbors saw anything," Chase reiterated. "Several of them were home at the time of the murder, and I can't imagine Mike would have been murdered quietly. Judging from the scene at the garden house, he must have put up quite a big fight. And yet nobody heard anything. It seems almost incredulous to me."

"Well, that's how it happened," said Uncle Alec. "And let's not forget that we've got a third family member who ended up dead the night before. Drowned in the lake, even though according to Liam Cass she hated the lake and wouldn't ever go there."

Odelia shook her head. "Melissa Bell says that Allison wasn't afraid of the lake at all. She said she loved it there and they used to go camping when they were little and they were both in the same Girl Scout troop."

"So Liam Cass lied?"

"Or Allison lied to Liam."

"The lake wasn't the only thing she lied about," said Chase. "She also lied about not breaking up with him, and about going to NYU when, in actual fact, she had been accepted at the University of Texas, where she was going to stay with Melissa's aunt. She couldn't wait to leave and was going in just a few weeks, immediately after graduation, in fact, something else she didn't tell Liam."

"Or her parents," said Odelia.

Uncle Alec checked his notes. "One more piece of news. One of your colleagues found Allison's bike lying a couple of hundred yards from the outdoor center located on the bank of the lake. So that might very well be the spot where she went into the water."

"So she rode her bike there," said Chase. "To meet someone, maybe? Were there any messages on her phone?"

"Good point, Chase," said Uncle Alec, placing his hands flat on the desk. "I've got the data from all three of the Fishers' phones, though the information doesn't reveal much more than what we already know. Allison did indeed spend time by the ocean, according to the location data on her phone, then spent time at her friend Melissa's house until ten o'clock, then went home before leaving again at eleven, for some reason we don't know. She must have driven there, for it took her about half an hour to arrive at the lake, which puts her there at eleven-thirty. And then... nothing."

"No messages or phone calls?"

"Nothing. Dead silence."

"So she arrived there at eleven-thirty, and according to the coroner, she died half an hour later by drowning," said Chase. "Any signs of a struggle on her body or the location?"

Uncle Alec shook his head. "No strangulation marks on her neck, no bruising, no skin tissue under her fingernails... Almost as if she sat there for half an hour, then simply walked in and drowned."

"She was fully dressed," said Chase as he read from the same report on his phone. "Nothing was found on the bank except her bicycle, which wasn't locked. She still had her phone on her when she was found."

"Melissa said she was looking forward to leaving for Texas so much that she can't imagine she would have killed herself," said Odelia.

"So we can only assume that there must have been a second person there who pushed her head underwater until she was dead," said her uncle.

"Any luck tracking possible other phone signals in the area at the time of Allison's death?" asked Chase.

"Like I said, there's an outdoor center nearby where they organize boat tours, water skiing, surfing, hiking trips. They have a popular bar that was open last night, and that makes it hard to know who else besides Allison could have been out there."

"If she really was killed," said Odelia. "Though to be perfectly honest, I have a hunch that she was. Possibly even by the same person who killed her parents the next morning."

"If it was the same person, why didn't he use a knife, like he did with Mike and Chloe?" asked Uncle Alec. "Different MO means a different killer, in my opinion."

"And also, why wait until the next morning to go after Allison's parents? He could have returned to the house and murdered the couple in their bed. It would probably have been a lot less messy than having to chase Mike around the neighborhood, potentially being seen by half the block."

They were all quiet for a moment as they tried to picture the scene and piece together the correct sequence of events. Try as they might, though, they couldn't figure it out, as Odelia's next words confirmed. "I want to talk to the Fishers' next-door neighbors again. I just can't believe nobody saw anything."

"Okay, fine, talk to the neighbors," said Uncle Alec. "And while you're at it, talk to the people operating that outdoor center by Lake Mario. Maybe they also saw something."

CHAPTER 17

It wasn't long after the meeting concluded that Dooley and I walked out of the police station. We had been given clear instructions to find Bella and try to persuade her to tell us what she saw, and so moments later we were traversing her old neighborhood once again, in search of the Bichon Frisé.

As we glanced around, I thought that the Fishers' neighborhood resembled our own to a large extent: the same type of nice family homes, quiet streets with not a lot of traffic, the occasional cul-de-sac where kids could still play outside, nice front lawns, and more than one neighbor who stood mowing that same front lawn while glancing across the street at the neighbor's wife. In other words, your typical suburban pleasantville. Only in this particular pleasantville, something very unpleasant had taken place that morning. Though when we walked through the streets, I didn't get that impression at all.

"Life goes on, Max," Dooley told me, showing that at heart my friend is a philosopher.

"Yeah, I guess so," I said.

"Except maybe for the Fishers," he allowed.

"I wonder what will happen to Bella now."

"The Fishers will have relatives who can take her in," said my friend. "And if that's not the case, maybe one of their neighbors will."

We had arrived at the Fisher place and walked around the back to end up in the backyard. Police tape marked the spot where Chloe Fisher's body had been found, but no matter how hard we looked, there was not a single trace of Bella.

"Almost as if she's vanished from the face of the earth," said Dooley, his voice betraying his sense of growing discomfort about what could have happened to the little doggie. "You don't think…"

"What?"

"You don't think she was also murdered, do you? That the killer realized he had a witness and now he's gone and killed her too?"

"Humans don't bother with canine witnesses, Dooley," I reminded him. "Or feline. They don't think we pose any threat to them. And mostly we don't, except we can talk to our humans and tell them what we saw. But since the killer doesn't know that, he won't harm Bella. Or at least, I hope he doesn't."

"I hope so too," said Dooley. "She might not be very cooperative, but that doesn't mean we should wish her harm."

"Absolutely."

We walked along the back of the garden and wondered if the killer could have possibly escaped that way. Passing through the boxwood hedge that the Fishers had planted, we found ourselves in the backyard of a house on the next street.

"If the killer had escaped this way, these people would have seen him," I said, pointing to a man who stood at the window and was looking at us intently, and not in a welcoming way either. "And if he escaped the other way, one of those neighbors should have seen him."

"This case is baffling, Max."

"It sure is. Two brutal murders are committed in the heart of this pleasant little suburb, in broad daylight, and yet nobody saw anything? It's hard to believe the killer would take such a risk."

"Almost as if he knew that nobody would be home this morning."

"But that's just the thing, Dooley: some of these neighbors were home. Okay, so the Garcias across the street weren't, but mostly the others were."

"Didn't they have to go to work?"

"Some of them work from home, others the husband works but the wife doesn't, or the other way around. And yet nobody saw anything."

"Except Bella the dog."

"Except Bella, who won't talk to us."

"And who's conveniently disappeared."

It didn't take us long to determine that there wasn't much to glean. Odelia and Chase had promised Uncle Alec they would return to interview the Fishers' neighbors, but they were going to wait until dinner time when they were more likely to be home. And so we decided to shift gears and head into town. It took us about half an hour to get there, and when we did, we soon found ourselves in the presence of Kingman. But when we placed the voluminous feline in possession of the facts pertaining to the case, he was as baffled as we were.

"I'm baffled," he confessed. "A suspicious drowning, two murders in broad daylight and without any witnesses, and a canine witness that has gone missing." He frowned. "He wasn't taken in by the Amish, was he, like in that old Harrison Ford movie? Where the kid witnesses a murder and then has to hide in that Amish community so the killer can't find him?"

"I very much doubt that Bella has found refuge in the Amish community," I said. "Though it's possible, of course." No doubt stranger things have happened.

"Did you talk to some of the other canines there? Most of these neighborhoods are full of the creatures. You can't pass a house without some happy yapper trying to attach itself to your ankles."

"Oddly enough, this seems to be one of those neighborhoods that isn't rife with dogs," I said. "Though it's possible that we'll find them tonight when we return with our humans."

"Talk to the dogs," Kingman advised. "Or any cats you may find. The neighbors may be afraid to talk, possibly because they're worried that the killer might come after them next, but the pets won't have that problem."

"Yeah, I guess you're right," I said.

"Why would the humans be afraid, Kingman?" asked Dooley.

"Why? Because this is clearly a mob hit, and those mobsters mean business. If you squeal on them, you will find the head of a horse in your bed, and then next thing you know, a car will drive by your house and shoot you dead."

"I very much doubt this is a mob hit," I told our friend.

"Are you sure? Cause it sounds like that to me. Though of course, it could have been the boyfriend. If what you're telling me is true, he had his reasons to be upset with the Fishers, especially if they treated his girlfriend so badly."

"Allison was leaving her boyfriend," said Dooley. "So if he found out about that, he might have killed Allison rather than having to give her up."

"Allison even said as much to Melissa," I reminded him.

"But if he did end up drowning her, who killed Allison's mom and dad?"

"I'm telling you, it was a mob hit!"

"Mike Fisher was an ad guy," I said. "Why would the mafia murder an ad guy?"

"Because... he made them look bad? Maybe he made an ad for them, and it didn't work, so they decided to ice him and his wife?"

"The mob doesn't have ads made," I said with a laugh.

"Oh, yes, they do. All those mobsters have legitimate businesses as a front for the illegitimate ones. Those businesses, like restaurants, trash-hauling companies, casinos, construction companies, need to advertise, just like any business. So maybe Mike messed up, and now these mobster bosses decided to teach him a lesson by making him dead."

"Making someone dead isn't teaching them a lesson."

"It teaches all the other guys a lesson. Guys like this..."

"Bruno McIntyre?"

"Exactly! Now he'll think twice before messing up one of their campaigns. Lesson learned, profit made. It's all about the money with these people, Max. It's that simple." Clearly, he was baffled no more.

"I still don't see how murdering three people in cold blood is good for business."

"Two people. Allison Fisher drowned. It's unfortunate, but it happens. The fact that her folks got whacked this morning is just one of those coincidences."

"You think?"

"Of course! Now all you have to do is find these mobsters, and case solved. It's that simple."

"Are you sure?" said Dooley. "Because nobody in the neighborhood is talking."

"Omertà."

"Bless you," said Dooley.

Kingman grinned. "Omertà is the code of silence enforced by the mob. You talk, you die. So nobody talks, it's that simple."

"So if nobody is talking, how are we going to solve the case?" I asked.

"Find the dog, break the dog, solve the case," said Kingman.

Dooley made a face. "I don't want to break the dog, Kingman. Even though the dog isn't talking, I like the dog."

"You can't make an omelet without breaking a couple of eggs, Dooley. And you can't solve this case without breaking a couple of dogs. It's that simple."

"But the reason she's not talking is that she's traumatized."

"You always were a softie, Dooley. These are hard people you're going up against, so you need to toughen up, little buddy. Adopt the Dirty Harry approach and go in there guns blazing!"

"But I don't want to go in there guns blazing!"

"Then you'll never catch these mobsters. It's that—"

"Simple," I finished the sentence.

"See? Max gets it. As I see it, you only got the one witness, who's hiding out at the Amish constructing homes with Harrison Ford, who's in love with some local girl. So now you need to go in there, get that dog out of there, make her sing like a canary..."

"Why a canary?" asked Dooley.

"Because, Dooley. In a case like this, there's always a canary."

"Okay."

"Harrison gets the girl, you get the canary, and we all live happily ever after. Case closed!"

Somehow I had a feeling it wouldn't be that simple.

CHAPTER 18

Kevin Thomson was feeling a little frustrated. He had been staking out the Poole place all day now, listening in on conversations, but so far he hadn't picked up anything of note. Those cats were never home! He had no idea where they were, but they sure as heck weren't where they were supposed to be, doing what they were supposed to do: talking to their humans and providing him with some interesting stuff he could use against the Pooles.

He had hoped to collect more sound bites, but it was becoming more and more clear to him he'd have to wait until he could start work on the reality show he had tricked them into before he could actually gather enough evidence to expose them as the weird freaks that they were.

He paced the small attic room now, feeling like a prisoner in that confined and cramped space. Not to mention that it was so hot in there that he was sweating like a pig. If he managed to pull this off, he swore he was going to ask for a big raise. Though that might not even be necessary. If this reality show was a success, he might not even have to stay in his profession. He could quit his job at the *Chronicle* and become a TV producer instead. 'Keeping up with the Pooles' first, and then maybe a spin-off about that annoying grandmother, or a nature show featuring those horrible cats. He could think of at least a dozen different possibilities he could pursue, and the network would eat them up if his first show was a hit.

He had a lot riding on this idea, he realized, and so he needed a hit if he ever wanted to get out of this cramped space and move into a nice big villa with a swimming pool, a private in-house cinema, an ice rink, and all the accouterments of success that a hit show could bring.

He watched as the cats now came traipsing up, then disappeared behind the house. He knew they had access to the house through the pet door, and as he placed his headphones back on his ears, he listened intently to pick up a snippet of conversation between the cats and their humans. All he needed was one piece of conversation where the Pooles actually confirmed they could talk to their cats. It wasn't enough to record a bunch of weird cat sounds that either they or their cats were making. He needed one of them to say the words, on tape.

But try as he might, he didn't pick up anything. As usual there was a lot of meowing, but nothing more.

And so he took off his headphones and threw them across the desk. Looked like he'd have to wait until his reality show got going. With several camera crews following the family members around twenty-four-seven, they were bound to pick up something sooner or later.

Behind him, the old lady whose attic he was inhabiting suddenly appeared. "And?" she asked sweetly. "How are you doing, Agent Cooper? Have you caught the bad guys yet?"

He saw she was carrying a tray with a cup of hot sweet tea and a couple of home-baked cookies. The last thing he needed right now was hot tea, but since he didn't want to insult Mrs. Wilkinson, and in the process get kicked out of her attic, he graciously accepted the tray and placed it on the little table next to the cot that served as his bed. He'd told her his name was Gary Cooper and that he worked for the FBI and she had happily swallowed the story.

"Oh, I'm doing great, Mrs. Wilkinson," he said. "Thanks for the tea and cookies."

"Least I can do for my favorite G-man," said Mrs. Wilkinson, her face wrinkling into a wreath of smiles. She had approached the window and studied the equipment Kevin used.

"Please don't touch anything," he said. "It's all very delicate."

"Oh, absolutely," said Mrs. Wilkinson. "I wouldn't think of touching anything." She now stepped over to the telescope. "I see you're looking straight into the bedroom of Vesta Muffin," she said. She shook her head. "And to think I've lived across from these people all these years, and I had no idea they were enemies of the state."

"Well..."

She suddenly turned to him with some vigor, and he saw her cheeks had colored. "You have to stop them from doing these anti-American activities, Agent Cooper."

"Oh, but I will," he assured her. "I will catch them in the end."

"So is she a communist? Or a terrorist? Is she working on constructing a nuclear device?"

"I can't possibly tell you, Mrs. Wilkinson."

She held up a hand. "Of course. Top secret. But if she was working on a nuclear weapon that she planned to set off in this neighborhood, you would tell me, wouldn't you? Because if that was the case, I'd go to my sister's place in Massachusetts and take Sylvester with me."

Sylvester was the canary Mrs. Wilkinson possessed and of which she was extremely fond.

"I'm sure Sylvester doesn't like radiation," she said. "But then neither do I."

"I don't think anybody is fond of radiation," he said. "And if Mrs. Muffin was indeed planning to set off a nuclear device, you'd be the first to know, I promise."

"Oh, thank you so much, Agent Cooper," she said, clasping her hands together. "The day you picked me to set up your surveillance post was the luckiest day of my life. Imagine living across the street from Enemy of the State Number One and not even knowing it!"

A twinge of alarm shot through him. "You didn't... talk to anyone about this, did you?"

"Absolutely not!" she assured him. "My lips are sealed, Agent Cooper. You can count on me to carry your secret to the grave."

And with this slightly disconcerting message, she walked out again. He now turned up the speed on the fan Mrs. Wilkinson had gotten him after he had complained about how hot her attic room was. It didn't seem to do a lot of good, just moved the hot air around in a sluggish sort of way. And as he plucked his shirt from his sweaty back, he returned to his observation post to study the goings-on across the street.

Sooner or later, they'd have to discuss their strange habits. And when they did, on camera, he'd finally have started making progress on his secret mission.

* * *

REBECCA WILKINSON WALKED down the stairs with some effort and wondered, not for the first time, if she shouldn't

NIC SAINT

move out of this old house and into a nice flat, just like her daughter had been telling her.

"One of these days you're going to tumble down those stairs and break your neck," Belinda had told her on more than one occasion, which just showed how negative-minded the girl had become. It was living in New York City that made her that way. Those big cities with their pollution and their filth and those horrible crime-infested slums would give any person brain rot, and they had certainly given Belinda's brain a negative spin.

Though if it was true that Vesta Muffin was a terrorist and was working on a nuclear bomb, Hampton Cove wasn't a lot safer than New York.

She stepped out of the house now, but not before feeding Sylvester, her precious tweety bird, and receiving a tweet-tweet in return for her trouble.

As she carefully shuffled along the sidewalk, she couldn't help but glance up at Vesta's room, and a look of anger crossed her otherwise amiable face. A nuclear bomb indeed. And the crazy woman was probably going to set it off right here in the middle of this nice neighborhood where Rebecca had lived for over sixty years, ever since her husband Ben and she had bought the place and raised their daughter. Ben had died a couple of years ago from cirrhosis of the liver—he was always too fond of the drink. But she'd be damned if she was going to allow that evil old woman to destroy their lovely neighborhood with her bombs.

She met old Mrs. Tucker on the corner, and her friend must have noticed how she was looking, for she said, "But Rebecca, honey, you look positively dreadful!"

"It's that Vesta Muffin," she said, before she could stop herself. And then, figuring Mrs. Tucker wouldn't gossip since she was discretion personified, she told her friend all about that nice G-man who was staying in her attic room and who was keeping an eye on Vesta Muffin, a known terrorist with links to organized crime, who was building a nuclear bomb that could destroy their whole town and leave nothing but a smoking mushroom cloud behind. "But don't tell anyone," she told her friend, who looked as shocked and upset as she was feeling.

"Oh, absolutely not," said Aline Tucker. "I wouldn't dream of it."

"I hope this nice man will stop her. He likes my tea, you know, and my cookies."

"Well, he should," said Aline, who for some reason seemed anxious to get away. Probably she had shopping to do. Or maybe she had messages on her phone she needed to read. Most people Rebecca met these days were always looking at messages on their phones. The only messages she ever got were from Belinda, who had told her that these days everything that was interesting or important was to be found on the internet.

She could have told her that everything that was important was located right in her old mother's attic room! With Agent Cooper trying to save the world!

CHAPTER 19

Dinner time had arrived, but instead of sitting down for a nice dinner, Dooley and I found ourselves being scooped up by our humans and compelled to experience déjà vu when they returned to the Fisher place.

"Weren't we here earlier, Max?" asked Dooley when he happened to glance out of the window.

"Yeah, we were here only an hour or so ago," I confirmed.

"So... why are we back again?"

"Because this time we're going to interview the Fishers' neighbors, remember? Making sure they're home and sitting down for dinner? It's the best time to catch anyone since they're almost definitely home." Except maybe during the Super Bowl. Though I doubt they'd answer the door and be prepared to be peppered with questions at such an important time. They might even become homicidal themselves if they were prevented from watching Tom Brady or one of his successors doing what they did best, namely scoring touchdowns.

Dooley shivered now, and I understood why. Kingman

had been feeding us with stories of the mob, and so now Dooley was looking for an armed gangster behind every tree.

"Okay, we're here," Chase announced. "Let's do this, people."

"And cats," Odelia added with a smile.

He had parked in front of the Fisher place and now got out, glancing around himself and taking in the neighborhood at a three-hundred-and-sixty-degree angle. "Someone somewhere saw something," he said. "So let's get those witness statements in and solve those murders!"

And since he figured he had offered enough of a motivational speech, he headed for the house next to the Fisher place and stabbed a finger at the buzzer. Moments later, a balding man of about fifty years of age answered the door, giving us a quizzical look from behind thick glasses. "Yes?" he asked in a sort of high, reedy voice.

"Detective Chase Kingsley, sir, Hampton Cove Police Department, and this is civilian consultant Odelia Kingsley."

The man smiled. "You're a couple, aren't you? I've been reading your stories in the paper, Mrs. Kingsley, and I have to say it's an honor to finally make your acquaintance."

"Thanks," said Odelia. "It's an honor to meet a loyal reader such as yourself."

The man shone with contentedness at this unexpected privilege.

"Who is it, Marcus?" suddenly a voice boomed from behind him.

"The cops!" he bellowed back. "And two cats!" he added belatedly.

"Cop cats?" his wife shouted back. "Are you drunk again?"

He gave us an apologetic look. "My wife is kidding," he hastened to explain.

Moments later, the woman in question appeared at the door, and when she saw the collected company gathered there, she blinked. Like her husband, she wore thick glasses and had curly gray hair dangling in ringlets around her ears. "You weren't kidding," she said finally. "It is the cops... and the cats."

"We wanted to ask you a few more questions about what happened next door this morning," Chase said, deciding to put an end to all this crosstalk. The couple introduced themselves to us as the Millers, Marcus and Melanie, and the latter now nodded sadly.

"Yeah, the Fishers," she said. "Such a sad business."

"Very sad," her husband concurred.

"We liked them, didn't we, Marcus?"

"We liked them very much."

"The best neighbors. Always ready to let us borrow their lawnmower."

"Or their ladder."

"We don't have a ladder," Melanie explained. "So when our gutter needs repainting, we ask Mike if we could borrow his."

"He was always fine with it," said Marcus. "So nice of him."

"So very nice."

"They were a nice couple."

"Okay, so about this morning," said Chase. "Did you happen to notice anything out of the ordinary?"

The couple shared a look. "Nothing out of the ordinary," said Melanie.

"No, nothing special," said Marcus.

"You were both home?" asked Odelia.

"Oh, yes, we were. I work part-time," said Melanie. "At the community center."

"And I work full-time, but only three days physically at the office and two days from home."

"It's a neat arrangement," said Melanie. "That way Marcus

avoids the traffic, though we do spend a little more for heating and electricity, don't we, honey?"

"I get compensation. Not much, but something."

"Okay, so you were both home this morning, and yet you didn't notice that two of your neighbors were being murdered?" asked Chase, who was getting a little worked up.

Both Millers shook their heads. "Noticed nothing," said Melanie.

"Nothing at all," her husband said.

"Must have been a very quiet killer."

"Extremely discreet."

"You didn't hear any screams?" asked Odelia. "Or witness some kind of altercation?"

"No altercation, no screams," said Marcus. "So you can imagine our surprise when one of your colleagues told us what happened."

"So shocked," said Melanie, shaking her head. "Shocked and horrified."

"Very horrified. It's not every day that your neighbors are murdered in their own home."

"Their own backyard," Melanie corrected her husband.

"Well, Chloe was murdered in her backyard, and Mike in Jerry Garcia's garden shed," said Marcus, who seemed to be the kind of person who liked to dot the I's and cross the T's.

"Did you happen to talk to any of your other neighbors about what happened?" asked Odelia. "Maybe they saw or heard something?"

"Oh, we talked about it," said Melanie, "but no one saw anything either."

"It's the darndest thing," said her husband. "Odd how something like that just happens, and nobody saw a thing. But then I guess it's often that way in neighborhoods like ours."

"And what kind of neighborhood would that be?" asked Chase tersely.

"Well, quiet, I would say," said Melanie. "Quiet and peaceful."

"Except for the murder of the Fishers," her husband pointed out.

"Well, obviously. But apart from that, everybody likes to keep themselves to themselves and mind their own business. Our own little patch of peace and quiet in the middle of a busy town." She sighed contentedly.

"It is a wonderful place to live and raise kids," Marcus agreed.

"Do you have kids? Maybe they saw something?" asked Odelia.

"We do have kids, but they moved out a couple of years ago."

"Empty nesters," Melanie said with a smile. "That's us. And it's exactly the way we like it, isn't it, Marcus?"

"We love it," said Marcus. "The whole house to ourselves."

"Mind you, we love our kids."

"We adore them."

"Absolutely adore them."

"But it's nice to have some peace and quiet after all those years."

"Which is exactly what we get here in our little patch of paradise."

As we walked away, I could hear Chase curse under his breath. Clearly, he wasn't fully in agreement with this whole 'patch of paradise' business. He wanted nosy parkers, neighbors who were in each other's business all the time, who spied on each other, and maybe even used their binoculars to look in through the windows to see what the Millers or the Coopers or the Parkers were up to. But apparently, that wasn't how the Millers rolled, which was bad news for the cop since a neighbor who keeps himself to himself makes for a pretty useless witness.

Unfortunately, as we went from house to house, variations of the same story reemerged over and over again. Nobody had seen anything, nobody had heard anything, the Fishers had been lovely people—absolutely lovely. Mike had lent out his ladder to one and all, and the gist of it was that by the time we had spoken to all the direct neighbors, we still weren't any the wiser about what had happened that morning, except now we knew all about Mike's ladder.

"They're very discreet, aren't they, Max?" said Dooley. "Very respectful of each other's privacy."

"A little bit too respectful, as far as I'm concerned," I lamented.

Chase and Odelia obviously felt the same way, for by the time we were down to our final neighbors, they both looked extremely frustrated. Our next potential witness was a young woman with pink hair who looked mildly amused by the presence of two police officers at her door.

"The Fishers? Oh, that's right. I heard all about that. Is it really true that they were murdered?"

"They were murdered," Chase confirmed. "So you wouldn't happen to have noticed anything out of the ordinary this morning, would you?"

She thought for a moment, then shook her head. "Nope."

"A scream, maybe? A car racing by? A person behind the wheel who isn't from around here?"

She thought again, then shook her head again. "Nope."

Chase sighed. "Why is it that two people were murdered and nobody saw anything or heard anything? Can you tell me that, Miss..."

"Foster. Chris Foster." She smiled. "I guess we're one of those neighborhoods where people simply don't seem to care as much about their neighbors as they should, the curse of the modern age, you know? People leave in the morning, get in their car to head into the office. Then at night they arrive home, close the door, and disappear behind their curtains to watch TV. I don't even know most of the people who live here, and I've been here ten years."

"Don't you think that's just horrible?" asked Odelia, who clearly couldn't imagine neighbors not talking to each other. Where we lived, the Pooles knew everyone on the block, and the neighbors knew them.

Miss Foster made a face. "I guess you get used to it? And it's not as if I don't know some of the people. Like, I knew the Fishers, for instance?"

"Don't tell me. Mike lent you his ladder from time to time?" asked Chase with just a touch of sarcasm.

"His ladder? Why would I need Mike's ladder?"

"No reason," said Chase dryly.

"Look, have you considered the fact that maybe the Fishers killed each other? That Chloe Fisher killed her husband, and then he killed her?"

"You mean like a murder-suicide?"

"No, like a murder-murder. It was pretty obvious that those two hated each other. I mean, sometimes I could hear them screaming all the way over here."

"I think it's unlikely that that's what happened," said Chase. "Considering the way they died. But I'll definitely take it into consideration," he added.

"You asked my opinion, and that's my opinion. Mike stabbed Chloe, only she didn't die straight away. It only made her angry, like the monster at the end of a horror story, so she got even by stabbing Mike. And eventually, they both died. Like in that movie *War of the Roses*, you know, where the couple trying to kill each other die in each other's arms."

"The Fishers didn't die in each other's arms," said Chase.

"Even in death, they didn't get along," said Miss Foster

with a wry smile. "Anyway, give it some thought, detectives. Pretty sure that's how it all went down."

We thanked her for her time, and I think we all felt a little bit frustrated by the lack of neighborly spirit, but at least we had one more theory to consider.

Though in all honesty, I had my doubts that Miss Foster's theory had any merit. It's a little hard to murder another person with a big knife stuck in your back. Unless Chloe Fisher was superhuman, of course. Though from most accounts, people seemed to think she was subhuman.

CHAPTER 20

Mrs. Edwina Malt was an older lady about Gran's age, and with her little white curls and pale blue eyes, she looked like a lovely person. She took us straight into her backyard, where she said she'd been gardening a little. As our humans took a seat at her cast-iron garden table on the patio, I thought her garden looked just about the prettiest of all the gardens I'd seen so far, with plenty of floral delight to feast the eyes on. Obviously, she took great pains to maintain it.

"Oh, it's my hobby," she said when Odelia complimented her on her flower beds. "I wouldn't know what else to do with myself if I didn't have my lovely little garden to attend to. Though my knees have been giving me trouble lately, especially when the days aren't as sunny as today. But I soldier on!" she said with a vivacity that belied her years.

"So, about the Fishers," said Chase, deciding to launch into his interview. Contrary to Odelia and her mom and grandmother, Chase isn't big on gardening and clearly wasn't born with a green thumb like the rest of the family he'd married into. "What can you tell us about what happened this morning, Mrs. Malt?"

"Such a sad business," said Mrs. Malt as her face clouded. "Allison was such a nice girl. She used to come round here from time to time, you know, to help out in the garden. But that was before Chloe forbade her, of course."

"Forbade her?" asked Odelia. "What do you mean?"

"Well, Chloe and the people from the neighborhood didn't get along all that well. Which was only to be expected, since she wasn't the easiest person to get along with. And so out of spite, she would exact little punishments to get back at them. She didn't like the fact that I refused to endorse her campaign to get elected for the town council, for instance, and so she told Alison that she couldn't come round here anymore. Though Alison did so anyway," she added with a smile of satisfaction. "Because that's the kind of sweet girl she was."

"Chloe was running for councilor?"

"Oh, absolutely. It wasn't enough that she lorded it over her own family. Now she wanted to give us all the benefit of her cruel and obnoxious personality by being elected for a seat on the council. She wanted us all to support her campaign, of course, but I, for one, flat out refused to put a poster in my window or a billboard in my front yard. Can you imagine having to look at that woman's ugly face every day? The horror!"

"Nobody told us about that," said Chase.

"They didn't? Oh, well," she said primly, then directed a kindly smile at her guests. "Would you care for a cup of tea? I just love a nice cup of herbal tea, don't you?"

"We probably should be going soon," said Odelia, keenly aware that the clock was ticking and that we needed to get home for the big family meeting.

"I'll have one myself," Mrs. Malt announced. "And I'll make an extra big pot. Then, if you change your mind, you can always have some. It's really delicious tea. I get it from a little shop in town that sells excellent blends. This one is called Summer Blossom, and it's my current favorite. It's got cinnamon, orange, and hibiscus." She disappeared into the house, and we heard some clattering in the kitchen, cabinets being opened and closed, and a water kettle going on the boil. Moments later, our hostess resurfaced carrying a tray. She had also brought three cups and saucers, and so despite their earlier stated anti-tea position, our humans quickly acquiesced and were soon sipping from the brew and making appreciative noises.

"Allison used to sit right where you are now sitting," she told Odelia with a sad smile. "Oh, she was such a lovely girl. I'd known her since she was born, of course, so I watched her grow into a fine young lady. Though I have to say I often worried about her, with the kind of harridan she had to live with at home."

"What I don't understand," said Odelia, "is that Mike didn't do more to protect his daughter from his wife's behavior."

"Oh, but he did. He absolutely did. I think it's safe to say he shielded her from most of it. And it's not that Chloe had always been like this. When they first moved here, Mike and Chloe were a fine young couple. And she quickly became very popular with her neighbors, as she went out of her way to cook for people when they were laid up with some illness or other malady, and was a keen dog walker or babysitter for anyone who'd ask. But then somehow she changed and became this moody, impossible person."

"What do you think happened that made her so?"

Mrs. Malt wrinkled up her nose. "I know exactly what happened. She fell off a ladder and fell on her head. And I don't mean this as a joke. That's literally what happened. She

PURRFECT ZOO

was cleaning out the gutter when she leaned out too far, the ladder slipped, and she tumbled down to the lawn below. If that ladder had been on the driveway, she might not have survived, but even so, she sustained a nasty concussion and was at the hospital for several days, under observation. And it was in the aftermath of her accident that her personality went through a radical shift. Gone was the kind-hearted, neighborly woman who could always be relied upon to help out at the neighborhood festival or sell raffle tickets. She became moody, withdrawn, and generally very unpleasant to be around. Spiteful too, like when she told Allison she couldn't come around here anymore. Though, like I said, Allison didn't listen and came anyway, causing her mom to throw a hissy fit on more than one occasion."

"Did you know that Allison was moving away to Texas?" asked Odelia.

"Yes, she told me about that. And it broke my heart to see her go. But she was probably right to get as far away from her mom as she could."

"What do you think happened to Allison, Mrs. Malt?" asked Chase.

"Well, the poor girl drowned, apparently," said the old lady as she put the delicate china cup to her lips for a sip. "It's all very mysterious to me, as I know for a fact that she was an accomplished swimmer. She was on the varsity for her school's swimming team and had won a few medals. So it's not as if she would have gone for a midnight swim and gotten into trouble."

"Do you think she was murdered?"

The old lady gave a sad smile. "Now if I had a crystal ball, I probably could have told you. But since I don't, I'm afraid I can't possibly tell you what happened. All I can tell you is that she will be sorely missed, as she was a lovely young lady, and we were all very fond of her."

"And what about the Fishers?" asked Chase. "Did you hear or see anything this morning that could shed some light on what happened?"

"The problem is that I live too far away from their house, you see. If I had lived right next door to them, maybe I would have been able to help you. But I'm too far away to have possibly seen or heard anything."

"The odd thing is that even the people who live right next door didn't notice anything out of the ordinary," said Odelia. "They didn't hear any screams, and they didn't see any suspicious activity. Doesn't that strike you as odd, Mrs. Malt?"

"I think it's a sad testament to the state of the world today, my dear. People don't seem to care anymore what happens right next door. I could be murdered in my bed tonight, and nobody would lift a finger to save me. It's not a pleasant thing to consider, but it's all too true."

It sounded a little bleak to me. After all, if we were murdered in our beds, I'm sure one of our neighbors would hear the screams and come running. At least I hoped they would. But apparently, here in this neighborhood, it was every man or woman for themselves.

"One other question, if you don't mind," said Odelia. "What did you think of the relationship between Allison and her boyfriend, Liam Cass? Did Allison ever mention him to you when she came to visit?"

"Oh, absolutely. Now there was a devoted young man," said Mrs. Malt, a smile lighting up her face. "He was the ray of sunshine that warmed Allie's heart. The way that boy went out of his way to be there for her and to try and make her happy. I've never seen a more devoted couple. They used to come over together sometimes, you know, to have tea on the patio just like you're doing now."

"A friend of Allison told us she was thinking about breaking up with him because she felt he was too clingy, and that she was even moving to Texas so she could get away from Liam."

Mrs. Malt frowned. "What? Oh, but that's nonsense. She would never break up with Liam. She loved that boy so much, and he worshipped the ground she walked on. He wasn't clingy. He adored her."

"Maybe he adored her too much? Apparently, he was so jealous that she felt suffocated and couldn't wait to end the relationship."

"I'm sorry," said Mrs. Malt, "but whoever told you that must have some other Allison Fisher in mind. The Allie I know would never break up with Liam. She told me herself that he was the love of her life, and if not for him, she wouldn't know how she could have coped living at home all this time." She smiled. "They were going to get married, you know. Allie told me the last time we met. They were going to elope together and get married, and then Liam was going to move out to Texas with her so they could be together always."

"Liam was leaving the family business?"

Mrs. Malt nodded. "He loved his dad and he loved his job at the garage, but when it came to Allison, he would have done anything, including quitting his job and moving to Texas. She said he was an excellent car mechanic and would have no trouble finding a job out there."

"But... did his mom and dad know?"

Mrs. Malt's pale blue eyes twinkled mischievously. "No, they did not. And he wasn't going to tell them either until he'd already left with Allie. Like I said, they were going to elope. It was the only way they figured they'd finally be happy together."

The teapot was empty, and of the home-baked cookies, many had been eaten, but Odelia had one final question. "The Fishers' dog Bella seems to have gone missing. You wouldn't have seen her by any chance, would you, Mrs. Malt?"

"Oh, that poor little thing. No, I haven't seen her."

"When you do, can you let us know?"

"Of course. Though I very much doubt she'd show up here."

"And why is that?"

"Because everyone knows that I'm not all that fond of dogs. A dog bit me once, you know, and it put me off the species entirely, I'm afraid to say." She glanced down at Dooley and me and offered us a smile. "Cats, on the other hand, are a different matter altogether. Lovely creatures, aren't they? And so graceful."

"Do you have cats?"

"No, I'm afraid not. I would love to have them, but so far I haven't been blessed with the privilege."

Odelia and Chase said their goodbyes, thanked the old lady for her hospitality and for offering us so much of her time, and then we left. As we did, I thought I heard a soft woofle just as she closed the front door. But of course, I could have been mistaken because Mrs. Malt had told us that she hated dogs.

CHAPTER 21

We hurried home so Odelia could be on time for the meeting she had called. It would mean that our humans would have to skip dinner, but that was the least of their concerns as the meeting was clearly more important to them than any dinner.

As we rushed over in Chase's squad car, the topic of conversation was quite understandably the recent interviews with the Fisher family's neighbors. "Okay, so according to most people we talked to, there wasn't a lot of interaction between the neighbors and the Fishers," said Chase as he steered the car through traffic with a steady hand.

"Apart from the fact that Mike's ladder was a very popular item," Odelia pointed out.

"Yeah, except for Mike's ladder. And the unanimous dislike of Chloe Fisher, and the fact that Allison was considered a real sweetheart."

"Who was also an excellent swimmer, which rules out the theory of an accidental drowning."

"Even excellent swimmers can drown," said Chase. "She may have gone for a midnight swim and gotten into trouble.

Though I have to admit that I'm favoring more and more the idea that she was also murdered. Possibly by her boyfriend Liam, if we give credence to Melissa Bell's story that Allison was breaking up with him and moving to Texas so she could be away from both Liam and her parents."

"But Mrs. Malt said that's all nonsense, and Liam was also moving to Texas to be with her."

"I think we should probably have another chat with Liam."

"And Melissa."

"It's all very complicated, isn't it, Max?" said Dooley. "First, Liam is staying here, and Allison is going off on her own, and now he's going with her to Texas. Can't these people make up their minds and decide which is which?"

"Someone is obviously lying to us, Dooley, and now we need to figure out who: Mrs. Malt or Melissa Bell. Though my money is on Melissa being the liar, though it's unclear what her motivation could be for lying to the police."

"It's punishable by law, isn't it, Max? Lying to the police?"

"It is," I confirmed. "And if Melissa lied, I can imagine Chase won't be happy about it."

We had arrived home and sneaked in through the pet flap while Odelia and Chase made haste to join the rest of their family in Marge and Tex's backyard. But since we weren't as keen as they were on this whole idea of skipping dinner, we wanted to have a bite to eat first. We found Harriet and Brutus on the couch watching television. It was a show called 'Living like Cats and Dogs,' with cats being interviewed about living with dogs, and vice versa. Though it was all staged, of course, and in cartoon form, so kids could enjoy the antics of both species. But it was funny enough that both Harriet and Brutus were laughing loudly.

"What's so funny?" asked Dooley with a smile as he hopped onto the couch.

"Oh, this is just so good," said Brutus. "It's done mockumentary style, with cats and dogs being forced to live under the same roof and being interviewed at regular intervals about how they feel about the other species. The things they're saying behind each other's back!"

The cats apparently had a lot of complaints about the basic lack of cleanliness of dogs, whom they accused of being smelly all the time, whereas the dogs complained about what they called the cats' essential laziness, spending all of their time sleeping on the couch. Dogs, on the other hand, with their unbridled energy, were always ready to play, fetch balls or sticks, and generally be a source of entertainment and service to their humans.

"I think being forced to play fetch simply is beneath our dignity," said Harriet. "Who in their right mind wants to fetch a ball, then be obliged to return it before the ball is thrown again? It's demeaning, Max. Not to mention dumb."

"It is a dumb game," I concurred as I watched on.

"And look at those dogs who jump into a pond to fetch a stick!" said Brutus, roaring with laughter as a dog now traversed a pond and was soon covered head to toe in pond scum. "Now, a cat would never do such a thing—never!"

"That's because cats are much smarter than dogs," Harriet said. "And also, we're not as easily swayed by such simple psychological tricks as being offered a treat when we perform a certain action."

"Shouldn't we join the meeting next door?" I asked. I had eaten my fill, and now I was determined to sit in at the big meeting so I could hear what decisions the family would reach in connection to the inheritance.

Harriet raised her chin. "Brutus and I talked about it, and even though we like the reality show idea, we have decided we don't want to have anything to do with the zoo business."

"But I thought you were excited about the reality show?" I asked. "You were going to call it 'Keeping up with Harriet?'"

"I know, but on further thought, it's not going to work. Not with three hundred cats."

"Yeah, can you imagine taking care of them?" said Brutus with a frown. "It's going to be chaos. And besides, why can't they be satisfied with us? Why adopt three hundred more?"

"They're going to eat our food," Harriet pointed out, "drink our water, trample all over our favorite spots, and generally make our lives a living hell. In fact, we've been saying that maybe we should put our paws down and tell them in no uncertain terms that if they want to adopt three hundred cats, they can say goodbye to the cats they already have, or at least to Brutus and myself. Isn't that right, sugar plum?"

"Absolutely, honey pie," said Brutus. "It's either those cats belonging to Odelia's cousin or us. There is no middle ground."

"And we would very much appreciate if you and Dooley side with us on this," said Harriet. "If we join forces, we still might be able to stop this plan in its tracks before it's too late and those cats will be here."

"The cats won't be living with us," I pointed out. "Odelia's cousin owned a zoo, and now they want to transfer this zoo to Hampton Cove, but that doesn't mean they'll stay at the house."

"What do you mean?" asked Harriet, giving me a look of confusion.

"They'll have to live in a kind of shelter," I said. "Odelia's cousin called it a zoo, though I can't imagine it actually was a zoo since a real zoo is designed to cater to visitors and offer a wide range of animals people can come and look at. If Cousin Beatrice only had cats, it wasn't really a zoo but a shelter."

"But we already have the pound," said Harriet, "and the shelter. So now they want to build another one?"

"Yeah, so Cousin Beatrice's cats can all stay together and don't have to be split up by being adopted by different families. She loved her cats so much she couldn't bear the thought of them being split up, which is why this zoo, as she called it, was her main stipulation. 'Get the five million and keep my feline family together, or the money goes to a local animal welfare organization that will do the same.' Only in that case, Odelia won't get any inheritance."

"I still think it's too much," said Harriet. "And besides, they haven't even thought to ask our opinion."

"And also, they'll be filming the whole process," said Brutus. "Which means they'll bring in a camera crew and upset our daily lives."

"Big intrusion," said Harriet. "Big, big intrusion of our privacy."

"Yeah, can you imagine this place suddenly crawling with camera crews and people filming our every move?" said Brutus. "It's going to be a living hell."

"It will turn you into a big star, Harriet," said Dooley.

This gave Harriet pause. "I know, but…" She eyed her partner uncertainly.

"You could be the star of the whole thing," I pointed out. "It's all about who captures the attention of the audience and who doesn't. If you played your cards right, this could be your big break. It could put you on the map."

Harriet's face had adopted a sort of dreamy look I recognized. It was the sort of look she often got when she dreamed of a big career as a major international star. To her, it didn't really matter if she became a star of the screen, big or small, a singing sensation, or if one of her YouTube or TikTok videos went viral and catapulted her into the stratosphere of fame.

She now turned to Brutus, her features softening and also her stance. "Maybe we've been too hasty. Maybe we should wait and see what this Sammie comes up with. Who knows, he could be our Ryan Seacrest. He could be the guy who puts this family on the map—and me!"

Harriet's mood had shifted again, as it often does, from one minute to the next, and Dooley and I shared a smile of satisfaction at a job well done. If Odelia wanted that money, as far as I was concerned she would get it—and our cooperation in the process.

Though I had the distinct impression that even though we may have scored points with Harriet, Brutus wasn't happy. His next remark was evidence of this. "I hate you, Max," he hissed as Harriet happily pranced away to join the big meeting next door. "You too, Dooley. I hate you both."

CHAPTER 22

"I'm not sure this is the right way to go about this," said Uncle Alec. "I mean, at the end of the day, this Cousin Beatrice, who I have to admit I've never heard of before, wanted to keep her cats together. So why not allow this money to go to this place in Alaska where they're probably better equipped than we are to take care of these creatures?"

"So you would honestly say no to a five-million-dollar inheritance?" asked his mother. "You are even crazier than I thought you were, Alec."

"It's simply common sense," her son argued. "We're not in a position to take care of three hundred cats, and besides, this whole idea about those cameras doesn't sit well with me. In fact, I think it's probably the worst idea anyone could ever have come up with. Which leads me to conclude that Cousin Beatrice was a crank."

"Are you calling our beloved family member a crank?"

"I am. For one person to keep three hundred cats tells me she was seriously deranged."

NIC SAINT

Gran was wagging a finger. "Careful now, Alec. You're treading on dangerous ground here."

"Okay, so you've got four cats. Which makes you a little eccentric, I guess, but three hundred? Come on, Ma. Obviously, the woman wasn't right in the head."

"And again with the slurs!"

When we arrived at the house, the meeting was already in full swing, and things were heating up. Though I have to say that maybe Uncle Alec had a point. And even though I was all for Odelia getting her inheritance, it was going to mean a big change, so in that regard, Brutus also had a point. The big black cat was still giving us the evil eye, so clearly we had stepped on his toes when we convinced Harriet to give the idea a try. But then I was determined to do what was right for my human, and if Odelia thought she stood a chance at pulling this thing off, I was all for it.

"Look, it's not difficult," said Odelia now. "All we have to do is say yes and then start thinking of ways and means of working out the practical arrangements, which I'm sure won't be as hard as we think it is. After all, if Cousin Beatrice could do it, why can't we?"

"I like your thinking, honey," said Marge. "And I think we owe it to Beatrice, who I've never heard of either, by the way, to take care of her beloved cats. If ever something were to happen to our family, God forbid, I'd feel much easier in my mind if I knew there was someone out there who would take care of Max, Dooley, Brutus, and Harriet. Wouldn't you?"

Uncle Alec considered this, then said, "Okay, four cats is fine, Marge. But three hundred? That's madness."

"All we have to do is hire the right personnel," said Marge. "And we already have a place we can put them: the Vesta Muffin Animal Shelter."

"We don't have the space, though," said Gran. "It's not equipped to handle such a big influx of animals."

"So we expand! With five million in the bank, there isn't a lot we can't do. And if we need more money, we sell the land that Cousin Beatrice already bought in Hampton Cove."

"We'd need permission from the town council for an expansion," Tex pointed out.

All eyes now turned to Uncle Alec's girlfriend, Charlene Butterwick, who grimaced. "Okay, so I understand you expect me to grant you permission simply because I'm a member of the family, but that's not how this works. You'll have to apply for permission from the zoning commission, and I'm afraid I don't have any say in these matters. Otherwise, every mayor would simply set up his or her pet projects and get them through the commission. That way corruption and favoritism lie."

"So you won't give us permission to take care of three hundred poor little kitties?" asked Gran.

"I would love to, but as I said, it's not up to me. But fill in the necessary paperwork and hand in your application, and I'm sure if it has merit, it will be approved in due course."

"And how long does it take, your due course?" asked Gran.

"I won't lie to you, it could take a while."

"A while being..."

"Months, probably. Years, maybe."

A murmur of disapproval rose up around the dinner table as family members all expressed their concern that this whole process could last this long. "And what are we going to do about Beatrice's three hundred cats?" asked Gran.

"We could always put them up at the house for now," Odelia suggested. Another roar rose up, which she quickly stemmed by holding up her hands. "We have to do something, and if the shelter can't accommodate them, and we can't build a zoo on this piece of land, we could put up a number of cats at the shelter and take in some here, and also ask around for possible guest families who can take care of them until this expansion of the shelter is approved."

"I agree," said Gran. "Anything to accommodate Beatrice's poor babies."

"Who's that?" asked Dooley suddenly. When I looked where he was pointing, I saw that a man hoisting a camera on his shoulder had suddenly appeared in front of the sliding glass door that looked out at the backyard. Next to him, another man stood, this one hoisting a large boom mic. And as a third man opened the door to allow the others in, I recognized him as Sammie Paston, the man handling Cousin Beatrice's estate.

"I'm sorry for the intrusion," said Sammie in unctuous tones, "but I thought we could get started on our show. Since this meeting is so important, I think it should be the kick-off, and then we'll take it from there." He now nodded to the two guys in his presence, who walked in and started filming. More members of the same crew now walked in, took up positions all around the dinner table, and aimed their cameras at the collected members of our family!

"Hey, what's all this?" Charlene said, rising up from her chair.

"This is the reality show we agreed upon," said Sammie. He held out a hand. "We haven't been introduced yet. My name is Sammie Paston, and I represent the interests of the late Beatrice Morris. As per the stipulations of her will, the five million dollars in her estate will only be paid out if her cats are rehoused, and to ensure this, she also demanded a reality show be shot as part of the rehousing of her clowder. And of course to show the world what wonderful creatures cats really are. Didn't Mrs. Kingsley explain all this to you?"

Charlene shot Odelia a critical look. "No, she did not."

"I was getting to that," said Odelia, looking slightly embarrassed. She now took Sammie by the shoulder and led him into the kitchen. "I thought we said we'd wait until I had organized a meeting with my family to decide."

"I know, but I figured the meeting was a good moment to launch the show. This way, the viewers at home will become familiar with the family, and the show will be off with a bang."

"I'm not sure about this, Mr. Paston," said Odelia.

"Sammie, please," said the executor of Cousin Beatrice's will. "If we're going to be working together, it's important to be on a first-name basis, wouldn't you agree... Odelia?"

Odelia nodded distractedly. "It's just that not everyone is on board with the idea."

"I'm sure you'll be able to convince them," said Sammie with an engaging smile.

And so the meeting recommenced, only this time it was being recorded for posterity, or at least the enjoyment of a potentially very large international audience.

I'm not sure if Odelia's family enjoyed being filmed, but at least one of those present absolutely loved the idea: Harriet was preening to her heart's content as one cameraman seemed adamant about focusing only on her and capturing every single moment of her presence.

It looked like a star was born.

CHAPTER 23

Dooley eyed me with a certain sense of uncertainty. "Max, why is that man pointing his camera at me?"

"Because we're now part of the show, Dooley. These people are going to film us, and then they're going to broadcast what they've filmed and turn it into a show for viewers to watch."

"But... is he going to follow me everywhere? Because I'm not sure I like being followed everywhere."

"Oh, you'll love it," said Harriet, who had quickly made a full turnabout from her original position that this whole inheritance business was a terrible idea, which had been a full turnabout from her even more original position that it was the cat's meow. "This is the life, you guys. Being at the center of attention twenty-four-seven. Sharing your hopes and dreams with the world. Connecting to people on a global platform. Oh, this is just so cool!"

We watched as she pranced away, her head held high, and then took up position in the center of a sunbeam, sending its rays into the living room, and took her time to pose for the benefit of the cameraman, who captured her with distinct relish.

Brutus had snuck up to us. "Okay, so maybe I don't hate you guys, but you have to admit it's a dirty trick you pulled on us, Max."

"I didn't pull this trick, Brutus," I told him. "This trick was already being pulled, and so either we went along with the whole set-up or we got sidelined."

"God," he groaned as Harriet struck another pose. "This is a nightmare. Are they really going to follow us everywhere?"

"Yes, absolutely everywhere," I said.

"Even into our litter box?" asked Dooley.

"Like I said before, I doubt it." Even reality shows have limits, after all. Not many, but some.

"I don't believe this," said Brutus. "And there are actually people out there who like this sort of thing?"

"A lot of people dream of being the star of their own show," I confirmed. "Though for us, it's different, of course. The show is only a means to an end. Cousin Beatrice wanted the world to witness if Odelia and her family would honor their commitments, and also to present her beloved cats in a new light, and this was the only way she figured she could pull that off."

"But I don't want them to follow me into my litter box, Max!" said Dooley.

"They won't actually follow you in, Dooley," I assured him.

"Okay, so we need to find a way to get out of this mess," said Brutus. "For Harriet, it's all fine and good. She loves this sort of thing. But the rest of us?" He arched a critical whisker. "I mean, I don't know about you guys, but I don't like being filmed all the time. It makes me feel self-conscious and frankly weird."

"Maybe we'll get used to it?" I said.

"I don't want them in my litter box, Max," said Dooley, reiterating his earlier position.

Odelia had joined the meeting again, and it was clear she faced stiff opposition from all those gathered around the table.

"I can't have my detective filmed when he's out investigating a crime," said Uncle Alec.

"And I don't want to be filmed going about my business of running this town," said Charlene.

"And I don't want to be filmed when I'm examining a patient," said Tex.

"They can film me," said Gran. "In fact, they can film me all the time. I think it's going to work wonders for the cause of senior citizens everywhere when people see a senior citizen like me doing all kinds of stuff they could only dream of."

"Like what?" asked Uncle Alec.

"Well, like waterskiing, hiking in the Adirondacks, scaling Mount Everest, going down the Niagara Falls in a barrel. You know, the kind of stuff I do on a daily basis, being the active, amazing, powerful woman of a certain age that I am."

"But you don't water ski," said Marge.

"And you have never hiked in the Adirondacks," said Tex.

"And you haven't scaled Mount Everest," said Uncle Alec.

"Or gone down Niagara Falls in a barrel," said Charlene.

"Shhh!" said Gran, pointing to the cameras that surrounded us. "I'm trying to project a positive image here. Create the kind of role model senior citizens in America deserve!"

"Oh, brother," said Uncle Alec as he shook his head.

The meeting dragged on, with the family members gathered around the table asking Sammie about a million questions about his intentions, what he hoped to accomplish with the show, if he already had contracts in place for the show to be broadcast, and on what network, and so on and so forth. At the end of the meeting, a vote was to be cast, and since it was important for the future of the entire family, including the feline contingent, Odelia wanted to make sure we also got to cast our vote. But with the cameras present, she could hardly get down on all fours and ask our opinion. That probably wouldn't go down well with potential viewers. She wanted us to become known as the family that had saved three hundred cats from being dispersed across the globe, but that didn't mean she also wanted us to be known as a family of weirdos who could talk to cats. And so she gave me a slight hint in the form of a nod of the head the moment the matter was being put to a vote.

It was all I needed to gather my friends, and so while the humans voted, we did the same. The results were mixed. Gran, Marge, and Odelia all voted for the deal, with Uncle Alec, Tex and Chase voting against. Charlene, Uncle Alec's fiancée and so officially a part of the family, cast the deciding vote and after long deliberation had also voted for the idea, as it would put Hampton Cove on the map and potentially attract lots of tourists. Grace could have added her own vote to the tally, but since she was a toddler she hadn't been included.

"The majority carries the vote," Odelia announced. "Motion granted!"

"This isn't a court of law, Odelia," Uncle Alec grunted unhappily, "and you're not a judge."

She now glanced down at the four of us. Harriet had raised her paw, and so had I, since my first loyalty is always to my human. Brutus had decided to vote against the idea, and Dooley... Well, Dooley wasn't sure.

"I'm not sure, Max," he said, breaking out into a panic. "How do I vote?"

"Well, you could vote with the majority," I suggested.

"Seeing as Harriet and I have voted for the idea, and Brutus against it, you could side with us."

"Or you could vote with me," Brutus suggested. "This is a terrible idea, buddy. These people will stop at nothing to get a close-up shot of your perky butt as you go about your business in your litter box."

Dooley shivered violently at the idea of a camera getting a close-up shot of his tush as he was performing his daily duty. "But I don't want them to film my perky butt while I'm doing a poo! Oh, the horror!"

"That's what they'll do," Brutus assured him. "The public wants blood and gore, and that's exactly what these people plan to give them—in spades."

"Nobody is going to film your tush," Harriet assured our friend. "Though they might want to film mine, of course," she said, shaking said tush with distinct relish.

"This is so hard," said Dooley, and glanced at me. "Max, what do I do?"

"Okay, so maybe you should vote against, if that's how you feel," I said.

Harriet gave me a look of distinct censure. "Max, what are you doing? We need to win this thing!"

"We will win it," I assured her and gestured to the table, where the vote had already been decided: four against three in favor of the reality show idea.

"Okay, so then I vote... against," said Dooley finally.

I gave Odelia the verdict, and she grimaced. Clearly, she had hoped for a little more support from her pets. But then it didn't really matter all that much since she now announced, "Looks like we're saving Aunt Beatrice's cats, you guys!"

"Yay!" said Gran, pumping the air with her fist.

And so our showbiz adventure began.

CHAPTER 24

Kevin was reasonably satisfied with the way the meeting had gone. The Pooles had ultimately decided in favor of the plan, as he had expected they would, with the women constituting the majority vote. They were often more practical than the males, and that five million dollars added to the household budget was no chicken feed, even if they had to tolerate the mild inconvenience of being followed around by a couple of camera crews for a little while. It hadn't been hard to find the crews since he had a lot of contacts in the world of media, given his position as a reporter for the *Chronicle*. So he had told them to point their cameras at the Pooles and to keep filming, no matter what. Now, as he studied the footage in the safety of his attic observation post, he cursed under his breath as he detected not a single instance where there was any communication happening between the human contingent and the cats—the reason he had set up this whole reality show and zoo business in the first place.

He leaned back and ruffled his hair as he thought deeply about his next move. The camera crews were still in there, and they weren't cheap, so his boss would soon start complaining about his budget going off the rails. But as long as he didn't have the smoking gun he needed, he had no other choice but to keep going.

Which posed another problem, one that he hadn't thought he'd ever face: where was he going to get three hundred cats? If he was going to prove to the Pooles that he was for real, and that 'Cousin Beatrice' was an actual person and had left them that money, he couldn't keep postponing the actual moment when her feline zoo arrived from America's Icebox.

He picked up his phone and tapped it against his front teeth for a moment, then dialed a number he knew by heart. It was a man he'd made the acquaintance of a long time ago, and whose services he'd required from time to time during previous assignments. Flakey, as the man's nickname was, offered anything anyone could ever need, for a price. If you asked him to deliver you a tank, you got it. If you needed to fly to Egypt to shoot a commercial on top of the Great Pyramid of Giza, he could make that happen. The man worked for a luxury travel agency and could provide anything to anyone at any moment—if the money was right.

"Kevin! What can I do for you?" the familiar voice caroled into his ear.

"I need three hundred cats, Flakey, and I need them now."

"Three hundred cats! What do you need them for?"

"Don't ask," he said with a sigh. "But I need them as soon as possible, and I need them delivered to the following address: Harrington Street 46 in Hampton Cove. Can you do that for me, Flakey?"

Flakey thought for a moment, but before long, the man named his price—a price that was steep but ultimately one that Kevin could live with, provided his gamble paid off, which he sincerely hoped it would. As they talked, he happened to glance out of the window and saw that his landlady was going shopping. With her shopping bag in hand, she passed Vesta Muffin on the street. However, instead of exchanging a greeting with her neighbor, Mrs. Wilkinson crossed the street, causing Mrs. Muffin to dart a curious look in her direction.

Kevin frowned. He didn't know why, but somehow the altercation gave him a powerful sense of foreboding.

* * *

Vesta Muffin was used to being regarded as the scourge of the universe. In fact, she had been in so many spats, great or small, with so many people in her hometown she'd stopped keeping a tally. If people, for some reason or other, disliked her and decided to forgo the pleasure of her company, that was perfectly fine with her. But the one person she had always been on good terms with was Rebecca Wilkinson from across the street. Which made it all the more disconcerting when Rebecca suddenly decided to cross the street the moment she saw Vesta coming. It simply wasn't Becca's habit to be mean to people or carry a grudge. She was probably one of the kindest people on the block. This made Vesta wonder what had suddenly gotten into her.

But since she essentially lived by the moniker of 'live and let live,' she decided not to read too much into her neighbor's strange behavior. Maybe she'd eaten a bad egg that morning or was feeling the strain of having recently received word that her joints weren't as up to snuff as she thought. People had their own issues to deal with, and when they acted out, it more often than not had nothing to do with you.

However, as Vesta wandered along, a camera crew following closely behind her, she came face to face with Aline Tucker when she rounded the corner. When she saw the look of horror on Aline's face, it was clear to her that something was seriously amiss this morning. Aline was a good friend of Becca's, so whatever had gotten into Becca to make her act this way may have transferred to Aline too.

"Vesta!" Aline said, looking at her like a deer in the headlights. "H-h-h-how are you? And w-w-what are these people doing with those c-c-cameras?"

"They're filming a reality show," said Vesta as she studied the woman closely. Aline's face had gone even whiter than usual, and if that wasn't pure horror in her eyes, Vesta wasn't the judge of character she prided herself on being. "My family is opening a cat zoo, and Hollywood is making a show of the process."

"A c-c-cat show!" said Aline.

"Not a cat show," she said. "A cat zoo." Though why Odelia's cousin Beatrice had insisted on opening a zoo with cats was still beyond her, to be honest. But then you can never account for people's eccentricity, especially out there in Alaska, where the cold must have affected Beatrice's brain.

Aline's eyes now darted all over like a ball in a pinball machine, clearly looking for a route of escape. The camera crew, meanwhile, was dutifully capturing the entire exchange, coolly observing every expression on Aline's face and every word she uttered.

"B-b-but your family already has cats," she said lamely. "Don't they?"

"Yeah, we've got four cats of our own," said Vesta. "But now we're going to add another three hundred that my granddaughter has inherited from her cousin Beatrice. She lived in Alaska," she added, figuring that explained everything.

"Oh," said Aline, as she brought a distraught hand to her face. "Alaska. Cats. Okay."

Vesta frowned. "Aline, why are you acting so weird all of a

sudden? And why did Becca just cross the street when she saw me coming? Did something happen that I should know?"

"Oh, no!" said Aline in a high-pitched voice. "Absolutely nothing happened!" Then she suddenly gave Vesta a pleading look. "Just... when you set off that bomb, could you give us advance warning? Considering we've been friends and neighbors for so long, it's probably the least you could do, right?"

"Bomb? What bomb? What are you talking about?"

"Well, that bomb you're building in your basement," said Aline, her eyes having widened to their fullest extent. "The nuclear device you're going to set off?" She stepped a little closer and lowered her voice. "Look, I sympathize with your cause, Vesta, whatever it is, but at least you can spare your neighbors, can't you? Maybe set off that bomb of yours somewhere else? Like New Jersey?"

It wasn't often that Vesta found herself at a loss for words, but this was just such an instance. Somehow she heard the words, but she couldn't quite fathom their meaning. And so, even as Aline's lips moved and she kept pouring out her desperate plea, Vesta found it very hard to convince herself she wasn't in bed dreaming.

Finally, Aline had finished and seemed to expect some kind of response from her. That's when she heard herself say, "Okay, I won't set off my bomb in this neighborhood, Aline, decreasing the value of my neighbors' real estate to such an extent they won't be able to sell."

"Oh, thank you so much, Vesta," said Aline, joy making her cheeks turn from their previous chalky white to a nice blossoming pink. "I appreciate it, and I'm sure our other neighbors will too."

And as she walked off, Vesta turned to the camera crew behind her and said, "Now that must be the weirdest exchange I've ever engaged in, bar none." But since the camera people had apparently received strict instructions not to engage with their target, they kept mum, which was pretty disconcerting in its own right, Vesta felt.

She walked on, wondering what other weird encounters she might have, when she almost bumped into a second camera crew, this one following around her four cats: Max, Dooley, Brutus, and Harriet. Clearly, they weren't used to all of this attention as they acted quite skittish. Even Harriet, who had been so much in favor of the whole idea, didn't seem entirely at ease with all the attention she was garnering.

"We're going to the dog park now," said Dooley emphatically, speaking directly into the camera, even though he should have known full well that nobody would be able to understand him. "We're going to say hi to our good friends Rufus and Fifi, and also to our new friend Marlin!"

"Yes, we are going to visit Rufus, Fifi, and Marlin!" Brutus said, also speaking very loudly and enunciating clearly. "And then we're going to return home and take a nap!"

"I like naps," said Harriet. "I like naps very much. And that's because I'm a cat, and cats like to nap." She now directed a stilted smile at the camera that came across as a rictus grin in Vesta's opinion, and she actually had to chuckle. The only one who didn't seem all that affected by the presence of the camera was Max, who simply went about his business as usual and mostly ignored the media circus that was following them around. Vesta would have asked him why they were going to the dog park, since it wasn't exactly their habit, but then she couldn't actually interact with her cats as she normally did, on account of those cameras following them all around. She didn't want to make a fool of herself on national television by being exposed as some kind of freak, so she kept mum.

"Gran?" asked Dooley now. "Are you also going to the dog park?"

But instead of answering, as she would have done, she simply gave him a smile, crouched down to tickle his ear, and said, "Aren't you a cutie pie?"

"Gran, why are you acting weird?" asked Dooley, giving her a look of concern. Then his eyes widened, just as Aline Tucker's had done. "Oh, no! You can't understand us anymore, can you? You've lost the gift of speech!"

"Cutie, cutie," she murmured.

"Gran, talk to me!" said Dooley. "Say something!"

"Cute, cute."

"Max, Gran can't talk to us anymore!"

"Of course she can," said Max. "But with these cameras around, she can't."

"But why?"

"Because they're filming everything she says, and if she utters a single word to us, viewers across America will think Gran is weird."

Well, she was weird, of course, Max was right about that. But that didn't mean she wanted the whole world to know. She gave the big blorange cat a look of appreciation. Amidst all this weirdness, at least one of them was keeping a cool head. She straightened again and said as cheerfully as she could, "I'm going to the dog park. I have this sudden desire to go and look at the doggies."

And so she set foot in that direction, and so did her small clowder of cats. If Max thought there was something of interest to spy at the dog park, she might as well tag along and see what he was up to. Also, she wanted to see if there were more neighbors who thought she was working on a nuclear bomb and hear their opinions about the perfect place to set off such a device.

CHAPTER 25

I have to admit it took a little getting used to for us to be walking around with a camera crew in tow. Apparently, the whole idea was for us to stay together, or else they would have had to deploy four camera crews to follow the four of us around, and already they had the rest of the family to contend with. But since basically I was only doing this as a favor to Odelia so she could get her inheritance, I had decided to largely ignore the cameras and just get on with things. Dooley wasn't as easy in his mind as I was, though, and neither were Brutus and Harriet. They kept glancing over to the camera people, and every time they spoke, they did so in a stilted way, making sure their words were picked up by the guy handling the big boom mic hovering over our heads at all times.

"So why are we going to the dog park, Max?" asked Dooley, speaking slowly and deliberately all the while. "Is it because you like dogs so much, Max?"

"Yes, Max," Brutus chimed in. "Do you like dogs so much you can't wait to spend time with them down by the dog park?"

"I like dogs," said Harriet. "I like dogs very much. In fact, I like dogs so much I'm really looking forward to meeting them at the dog park. That's because dogs are our friends."

"Dogs *are* our friends," Brutus confirmed. "We all like dogs, and dogs all like us."

"I also like dogs," said Dooley. "I like dogs very much. Don't you like dogs, Max?"

Oh, boy.

We had arrived at the park, and if I'd wanted to approach our friends Rufus and Fifi in a casual way, the presence of those cameras made that pretty much impossible. The moment we walked onto the premises, all those gathered looked in our direction, wondering why a camera team would be following four cats around, and then a second camera crew would follow Gran around. I guess we were the circus now, and the circus had come to town.

Gran immediately made a beeline for her neighbors Ted Trapper and Kurt Mayfield, who were accompanied by Robert Ross. But if Ted, Kurt, and Robert were happy to see her, they didn't show it. Instead, they merely goggled at her, and when she approached, seemed disconcerted to a great extent.

"What's with the cameras?" asked Kurt with a frown.

"It's for a reality show they're doing on us," Gran explained. "It's a long story, and I'm sure Odelia will write about it in that paper of hers. So how are you doing, fellas?"

But the fellas weren't buying it. "I don't want to be filmed," Kurt immediately stated.

"Yeah, don't you need our permission or something?" asked Ted.

"I'm not sure I want to be filmed either," said Robert Ross.

"They won't use the footage if you don't want them to," Gran explained. "They'll simply edit it out. Or maybe they'll blur your faces or something. Make you look like pink blobs."

"And also change my voice," Kurt insisted.

"I don't mind being in the show," said Ted as he patted his hair. "Will this be on national television?"

"I'm not sure," said Gran. "Odelia is the expert. It's her show. The rest of us are simply along for the ride."

"Oh, okay," said Ted, putting on his best smile for the camera. He cleared his throat. "Have you ever felt like you could be saving a lot more on taxes than you are now? Well, if you do, call Ted at Number Crunchers and Sons. We'll provide you with all the best solutions so you can save big on taxes. Tailor-made offers, for businesses large and small, at Number Crunchers and Sons. Call us today. Or shoot me an email at ted@numbercrunchersandsons.com."

"What are you doing?" asked Gran.

"Well, I'm talking to the camera," Ted explained. "Though it would be nice to know if this is local television or national. I have a different pitch if it's for a national audience."

"God, Ted," said Kurt as he shook his head.

"What?"

"Our humans are acting a little weird, Max," said Dooley.

"I think everybody is acting a little weird," I told my friend.

"It's those cameras," said Harriet. "They make me feel self-conscious, you guys. I don't know how these Kardashians put up with it."

"I guess you get used to it after a while," said Brutus.

"I hope so, cause I'm not sure I can keep smiling like this," said Harriet. "My cheeks are hurting already!"

"I didn't even know that cats could smile," said Dooley.

"Well, I can," Harriet pointed out. "And you should too, Dooley. It's the only way you're ever going to become a major star. Stars smile, losers frown."

"But I don't want to become a major star," said Dooley. "It's the reason I voted against this reality show business, remember?"

"Same here," Brutus grumbled. But then he caught sight of the camera that was pointed at him, and he straightened his posture. "We're at the dog park now," he announced in a faux chipper voice. "Where, as you can see, there are many dogs of different varieties. You've got your Pomeranians, your Chihuahuas, your Pekinese, your Poodles, but also your bigger canines like this very handsome German Shepherd over there, for instance. All of these fine dogs are having a great time at the dog park." He paused. "And so are we."

While my friends were busy entertaining a national audience, I decided to amble over to Rufus, Fifi, and Marlin, who were shooting the breeze near the dog toilet.

"What's with all the cameras, Max?" asked Fifi as I joined them.

"Oh, it's something Odelia has decided needs to be done. Something to do with an inheritance she hopes to receive. Five million dollars, and all she has to do is set up a zoo for cats and allow these camera crews to follow us around for a certain period of time."

"It's pretty neat," said Rufus. "I wouldn't mind starring in my own reality show."

"Well, you can join ours," I said. "And then once you become a breakout star and capture the attention of the audience, you'll probably get a deal for a spin-off."

"Oh, so that's how it works, is it?"

"Absolutely." And since the topic of this reality show wasn't really all that fascinating for me, I addressed Marlin, the real reason I'd set paw for the dog park on this fine evening. "So I remember that you told us that your human wasn't happy with the Fishers? Chloe and Mike? That she thought Chloe was being abusive to her dog and she disliked her for that?"

"Yeah, that's right. But if you're trying to imply that Robert or Kimberly murdered the Fishers because they felt that Chloe Fisher wasn't being nice to her dog, I can tell you right now that you're meowing up the wrong tree, Max. Kimberly may be passionate about dogs, and she may hate dog haters, but that doesn't mean she would go around murdering them."

"No, I get that," I said. "But what I was actually wondering is if maybe Kimberly may have decided to save Bella and has taken her in and given her shelter?"

Marlin smirked. "I like your thinking, Max, but I can tell you that she hasn't."

"So have you—"

"Seen Bella? No, I haven't. Though I can certainly understand why she would have disappeared. If I had to live with these people, I would run away too."

"She only disappeared after her humans were killed," I pointed out. "So it wasn't as if she was actually running away from the abuse. But it's true that I very much would like to talk to her again since I believe she's in possession of vital information that could lead to the arrest of her humans' murderer."

"Look, if she did see the killer, she's unlikely to come forward, is she? She's probably terrified they'll come for her next, so she won't disclose any information that could lead to their arrest."

"Poor Bella," said Rufus. "What a terrible ordeal she's had to go through."

"Oh, I'm sure Bella has already found herself a new benefactor already," said Marlin. "Someone who's been taking very good care of her."

I frowned at the dog. "And you wouldn't happen to know the name of this person, would you?"

Marlin gave me a sly smile. "Even if I did, I couldn't tell you, Max."

"Well, you should, Marlin. It's always a good idea to cooperate with law enforcement."

"No comment," said Marlin.

I turned to Rufus and Fifi, my old canine friends and neighbors. "Is there anything you guys would like to tell me?"

But they both shook their heads, even though Fifi looked a little uncomfortable. Somehow, I had the impression they both knew where Bella was and were simply refusing to tell me.

"I'm sorry, Max," said Fifi finally. "But we are all sworn to secrecy."

"All dogs in all of Hampton Cove? You've got to be kidding me."

Rufus shrugged. "It's a dog thing, Max. We like to stick up for our own."

"I know this may come as a surprise to you, Max," said Marlin, "you being a cat and all, and cats not exactly being known for their solidarity, but dogs bond together, you know. We rally around our own and look out for each other."

"I'm not trying to trick you," I said. "I just need to talk to her."

"No can do," said Marlin decidedly. "I'm sorry, Max, but that's my final word on the matter. And now please move along. You've got your show to star in, and we have dog business to discuss. No cats allowed, I'm afraid."

And so, for the first time in a long time, I was being cast out of this select canine company just because they wanted to protect the witness of a crime!

But there was nothing I could do. And even though both Fifi and Rufus gave me apologetic looks, I still felt obliged to move along and let the dogs talk shop, no doubt discussing ways and means of further protecting Bella.

As I turned to the others, they all gave me curious looks. But when I shook my head, indicating my gamble hadn't paid off, they sagged a little. It looked like we'd have to solve the Fishers' murders on our own, without the benefit of our star canine witness who had successfully evaded capture and was being protected by her canine friends.

"But why, Max," asked Dooley. "Why wouldn't Fifi and Rufus cooperate?"

"Because they seem to feel that canine loyalty trumps any loyalty they might feel towards us, Dooley," I said.

"It's not fair," Brutus grumbled. "We've been neighbors and friends for how long now? And still, they refuse to cooperate with us? It's simply beyond the pale, Max."

"I know, but there's nothing we can do to make them talk," I said.

"Well, there is," said Harriet. "If we tell Odelia that Fifi and Rufus are refusing to cooperate with the investigation, she can put pressure on their respective owners to make them. For example, they could stop feeding them."

"Oh, that's low," said Brutus with a grin. "But I like it."

"Or they could stop taking them for their dog walks."

"Even lower. And I like it even more!"

"Or they could lock them up in their respective doghouses."

"Honey bunch, I love you so much right now!"

"Just a couple of suggestions to put some pressure on these treacherous canines," Harriet said with a shrug.

"I'm not sure this is the way to go," I said.

"It's mean, Harriet," said Dooley.

"So? They're being mean to us by refusing to cooperate. An eye for a doghouse."

"I don't think it would make a lot of difference," I said.

"Even if Kurt and Ted decided to go along with the idea, which frankly I don't think they would, no amount of pressure we bring to bear on those dogs will make them crack. That's just what dogs are like: loyal until their last breath. That's why humans love them so much."

"Yeah, cats don't have that," said Brutus. "At least not most cats," he hastened to add when he realized he was disparaging the good name of cats everywhere.

"I'm loyal," said Harriet. "Especially when Marge feeds me some of that prime beef she's been buying lately."

"I'm also loyal," said Dooley. "Though I wouldn't harbor a murderer. At least I don't think I would. Unless this murderer murdered my human's murderer. Then maybe I'd harbor this murderer."

"You mean, the murderer of our human's murderer is our friend?" asked Brutus.

"I guess so," said Dooley after a pause.

And since I felt we'd exhausted the topic, we decided to head back to the house and give the bad news to Odelia that we wouldn't be able to lay our paws on Bella any time soon.

CHAPTER 26

Odelia was happy that the family meeting had gone so well, but since her husband, her uncle, and her dad had all voted against the reality show idea, she felt she had some fences to mend. Her first opportunity to do so was when she arrived home with the camera crew in tow and found her husband sitting on the couch, looking glum. So she turned to the cameraman and the boom mic operator and asked them to switch off the camera and give them some privacy.

"Sorry, ma'am," said the cameraman, "but we've got strict instructions to keep filming."

"That may be so, but I want to have a quiet word with my husband now, so if you could please leave?"

But the guy shook his head. "I've got my orders. And if you don't like them, you'll have to take it up with Sammie Paston."

She shared a look with Chase, who shook his head disgustedly. Clearly, he wasn't a big fan of this reality show business. So she took out her phone and called Mr. Paston, the executor of her cousin's will and now also TV producer.

"I would like you to call off your camera crews," she told him. "I want a quiet word with my husband, and I can't do that with cameras present."

"I'm sorry," said Sammie. "But it's all part of the agreement: those camera crews will keep following your family around until after the zoo is open for business. Those are the terms of the agreement, Odelia, and I can't change them. Unless you want to forfeit the inheritance?"

She grimaced. "You're playing hardball, Sammie. All I want is a few moments of privacy. Is that so much to ask?"

"It is since it would negate the terms of the agreement."

"Fine. If that's how you want to play this—"

"Look, I don't enjoy having to be the bad guy here, but you knew the terms when you signed the agreement. So let's all calm down and try to make this work."

She shook her head. "Okay, fine," she said curtly and rang off. When Chase looked up, she gave him a quick shake of the head. She could see a vein starting to throb in his right temple, a clear sign he was starting to get a little worked up by this new reality they were in. And she could also tell that his hands were itching to show this cameraman and his boom man the door. But since they had signed the agreement, and they did have an inheritance in the balance, much to her relief he decided to remain seated and allow the shoot to go ahead.

It also meant she wouldn't be able to communicate with her cats, which was inconvenient, especially since they were in the middle of a murder investigation. Just at that moment, the four cats walked in through the pet flap, also looking glum, and before long, the door opened, and the camera crew tasked with trailing them also walked in. So as they now sat on the couch, with three cameras pointing at them, she suddenly felt very hot under the collar indeed. It was certainly a challenge to try and behave naturally with so many eyes on them.

"Okay, so we talked to Fifi and Rufus," Max said, "and also Marlin, who is the Rosses' dog and new in the neighborhood, and they are refusing to tell us where Bella is, even though I'm sure they're perfectly aware of where she could be holed up right now."

"Canine solidarity they call it," said Brutus, as he eyed the camera with a disdainful eye.

"The murderer of my murderer is my friend," Dooley explained, even though Odelia had absolutely no idea what he meant by that.

"Do you think my hair looks nice this way?" asked Harriet as she fluffed up her fringe. "Please don't film me from that side," she told the cameraman. "Only film me from my left. It's my best side."

"This is a nightmare," Chase said.

From the kitchen, Grace now came toddling up and crawled onto Odelia's lap. She babbled something they didn't understand, and Odelia gave her a peck on the cheek. Even though the cats could apparently talk to Grace already, Odelia couldn't, and probably wouldn't for a little while, until she had greatly expanded her vocabulary. It was odd that she would be able to talk in the cats' language and not in her own, but those were the peculiarities of their line of heritage. Possibly she had been the same way, though Mom claimed not to remember.

"We have to talk about the case," said Chase emphatically. "But we can't do it with those cameras present."

"I know," said Odelia with a sigh. It was an aspect of the matter she hadn't considered, even though obviously her uncle had, and Chase. "So maybe you and Uncle Alec can discuss the case at the station tomorrow? You wouldn't be surrounded by cameras there, surely?"

Chase arched an eyebrow. "If they follow me into the station, I'll arrest them. And I'm not even kidding." It could have been Odelia's imagination, but she had the impression that the cameramen all gulped a little at this shot across the bow.

The door now opened and her grandmother walked in, looking slightly dazed. Behind her, a cameraman and boom man followed. "It's just the weirdest thing," she now said. "As I was walking along the street just now, Jane Doyle accused me of building a nuclear bomb in my basement. She told me I shouldn't set it off here but take it to California and get rid of those annoying Californians. And when I met Aline Tucker earlier, she pretty much told me the same thing, only her suggestion was to wipe out New Jersey. I don't know what's wrong with people these days, but they all seem to think I'm building a nuclear bomb for some reason."

"So are you?" asked Chase. "Building a nuclear bomb in your basement?"

Vesta stared at the cop. "Not you, too!"

Chase grinned. "I'm just kidding. I know you don't have the chops to build a bomb, Vesta. Though if you did, maybe you could use it on producers of reality shows more concerned with their ratings than police detectives trying to do their jobs."

The cameramen gulped some more, but their cameras kept on rolling, whatever Chase said. And since it's hard—and possibly illegal—to discuss an ongoing murder case in front of no less than four camera crews, Odelia decided to change the topic and turn on the TV instead. A nice quiet evening at home with the family would be just what the viewers wanted to see, she reckoned. Though when they had settled in and were enjoying the preliminary stages of a movie, suddenly one of the cameramen piped up, "Can't you make this a little more juicy?"

"What do you mean?" asked Gran.

"Well, you know. Give the people what they want."

"And what is it that people want?" asked Odelia.

"Oh, you know, fights, arguments, screaming and shouting, gossip... the usual."

They all shared a look, and even the cats looked confused. "You want us to have an argument?" asked Chase.

"Absolutely. Arguments keep people glued to their couches. A boring family in front of the TV doesn't. It will put people to sleep."

"Maybe people should be put to sleep," Gran suggested. "It would make for a nice change from suffering insomnia."

The cameraman grimaced. "We're not in the business of putting people to sleep or making them change the channel, Mrs. Muffin. We're in the business of creating exciting television."

"So what, you want me to throw a plate or something?"

"Yeah, sure, why not? Or you could start screaming abuse at your granddaughter. Or give us the latest gossip from the neighborhood. Anything to keep those ratings up, you know."

"Okay," said Gran, and picked up the cup that was placed on the coffee table, then threw it at the cameraman's head.

"Hey!" said the guy, ducking just in time. "What do you think you're doing?"

"Just what you told me to do. Throw stuff."

"Not at me!"

But since Gran seemed to have a good thing going, and had derived a certain satisfaction from throwing that cup, she now picked up another cup and threw it at the boom man. It crashed into pieces on the wall behind the guy.

"Please stop destroying my tableware," Odelia said.

"If you want to throw something, throw some of the cutlery," Chase suggested.

"Oh, good idea!" said Gran, and headed into the kitchen to grab some of the knives and forks from the kitchen drawer.

The camera crews, who saw the danger lurking on the horizon, shared looks of unease but decided to stick around regardless. Their sense of professional honor was clearly stronger than their sense of self-preservation. But just when Gran was gearing up to practice her throwing skills, Odelia's mom and dad walked in, followed by their own camera crew, and stopped Gran dead in her tracks. They had brought along wine and snacks and now placed them on the coffee table, with Dad announcing, "Well, isn't this just the life? Our regular family night at home, enjoying each other's company as a family. Because that's the kind of family that we are. The family that likes to spend family time together. As a family."

Odelia frowned at her mom, who merely shrugged and mouthed, 'Your father's idea!'

Dad sat down on the couch, next to his son-in-law, and announced with a wide smile, "Patients have been coming to see me for over twenty years, and it's always been my great honor to treat them. Whether they're suffering from a sprained ankle or something more serious like gastritis or arthritis, I try to help them to the best of my ability. Two thousand positive Yelp reviews, two decades of practice, and thousands of satisfied patients don't lie. When you're in need of medical assistance, Tex Poole is your man. Tex Poole, family doctor, looking out for his family of patients twenty-four-seven. Tex Poole, the doctor with a heart for his patients. Find me at texpoolefamilymedicine.com. Because a healthy family is important."

"Dad, what are you doing?" asked Odelia, much surprised.

"Oh, nothing," said Dad casually as he opened the bottle of wine and poured himself a glass. "Just a nice evening at home with my family, you know. Because Tex Poole, family practitioner, is a family man at heart. So from my family to yours, here's to your health." He took a swallow from his glass, then spat it out again. "What's this?" he asked his son-in-law.

"Wine vinegar, Dad," said Chase with a grin. "I think you took the wrong bottle."

But Dad was nothing if not determined. So he plastered a smile onto his face. "As my son-in-law has just demonstrated, family helps each other. Family is there for one another in their time of need. And at the home of Tex Poole, that is doubly true."

Odelia whispered to her mom, "I thought he was against the reality show thing?"

"He's changed his mind," Mom whispered back. "He said he's found a way to make this work for us."

"Looks like he has," said Odelia as she watched her dad morph into the perfect salesman. Though if she were a viewer, she'd probably think twice about approaching Tex Poole with her medical issues. The man looked slightly—or a lot—deranged, to be honest. These cameras had a bad effect on him.

So as the family now sat together on the couch, all trying to look their best while facing no less than five camera crews, Odelia was starting to suspect this reality show just might be a bad idea. She suddenly felt a newfound respect for prisoners of war facing the firing squad.

CHAPTER 27

In spite of our predicament, or maybe because of it, the four of us decided to go to cat choir. It might provide us with the distraction we needed and offer us an opportunity to unwind in the face of the setbacks we were facing. A murder investigation is never an easy task, as murderers are typically reticent people and don't enjoy being exposed for the crimes they have committed. And to unearth their identities while being followed around by a couple of cameras makes things extra tricky.

And so, as we trotted along in the direction of the park, with our trusty camera crew in tow, Brutus grumbled, "Do these people never sleep?"

"I don't think so," said Harriet. "They have to be filming all the time, just in case they catch something juicy that will have people glued to their television sets, just like that cameraman explained back at the house earlier. They want people fighting and getting all riled up."

I have to say I'd never seen our humans look more miserable than when being faced with all of those cameras aimed at them, capturing their every moment and picking up every word they said. It probably wasn't a pleasant experience for them, as it wasn't one for us either. But at least we could chat freely and nobody could understand a word we said. Even though Brutus and Harriet and Dooley still seemed to labor under the misapprehension that they did.

"Okay, so now we're going to cat choir," said Harriet for the benefit of the camera. "It's a fun way to relax after a long day and also for cats to practice their unique skills as talented and creative artists. I, for one, think there should be a cat choir in every town in the country, and I feel lucky to be a part of it."

"Cat choir is a choir with cats," Dooley explained slowly. "Which means it's a place where cats come to sing."

"Yeah, and we have an actual conductor in the form of Shanille," said Brutus. "Who is just an amazing conductor."

"Shanille is amazing," said Harriet, "but it's the talented cats that cat choir is made up of that make the real difference."

"But sugar plum, the captain is the one who steers the ship in the right direction," Brutus argued, "so it stands to reason that cat choir's conductor would be the most important cat in the choir."

"I beg to differ, sweet pea," said Harriet, glancing at the camera and offering her most radiant smile. "Cat choir would be nothing without the talent of its members. Members like me, who make all the difference. Anyone can swing their paws and pretend they're an artist. But it takes a special skill to sing your heart out every night and entertain millions."

"There's probably more that goes into being a conductor than just swinging your paws," said Brutus.

But since we had arrived at the park, they decided to put

their discussion on the role of Shanille in the freezer for now. Shanille now walked over and frowned when she saw the camera crew, who had put on their lights since it was pretty dark at the playground where we like to rehearse.

"What's going on here?" she asked. "Who are these people and what are they doing here?"

"This is our camera crew," Harriet explained. "They're filming us for the purposes of creating our own reality show. It's going to be called 'Keeping up with Harriet,' and it will feature me and my friends."

"I don't think it will actually be called that," said Brutus, but Harriet quickly shut him up.

"So this is Shanille," Harriet spoke into the camera. "She is our conductor, which means she's the one who keeps the tempo, I guess, and generally makes sure our members don't sing out of tune."

"Oh, but a conductor does so much more than that," said Shanille, who was preening a little before the camera. "We select the songs, we create the harmonies, rewrite the score with the four different voice types in mind: the sopranos, the altos, the tenors, and the bass singers. And then of course we—"

"Yes, yes, yes," said Harriet, giving Shanille a slight shove and retaking her position in front of the camera. "The most important person in any choir is, of course, the lead soprano, since the lead soprano carries the melody. In fact, it's probably more accurate to state that the lead soprano creates the sound. Without her, there is no choir. So, in that sense, you could actually say that I am cat choir. Or as the French like to say it: cat choir, *c'est moi.*"

Shanille now gave Harriet a shove, though not as gently as Harriet had done. Harriet was cast aside and actually toppled over. "Cat choir is me," said Shanille in no uncertain terms. "I created cat choir, and I created the sound. Sopranos are replaceable, especially lead sopranos, who are just the worst. Prima donnas, every single one of them. But as we all know, a conductor is unique. Without me, cat choir wouldn't exist. It's as simple as that."

Suddenly, a sort of screech sounded behind me, and a whirlwind or tornado descended upon the scene and hit Shanille head-on. Before we knew what was happening, Harriet had tackled Shanille, and the two cats were fighting like... well, like cats and cats, I suppose.

"Ladies, ladies," said Brutus, trying to intervene. "We're all friends here."

The cameras picked up the cat fight with relish. Now this was the stuff people tuned in for, their operators seemed to think. This was the good stuff!

"Why are Shanille and Harriet rolling over the ground fighting, Max?" asked Dooley after a moment.

"Because they don't seem to agree on the respective roles of conductor and lead soprano," I said, "and their relative importance to the choir."

Fur was flying, and loud screeches filled the air. It wasn't all that different from our usual rehearsal, especially Harriet's caterwauling, which was all too familiar to long-time cat choir members like us. Most of cat choir had gathered around and watched with a sense of surprise. But then suddenly, one cat stepped to the fore, screaming even more loudly than both contestants and causing them to give pause. It was, of course, Clarice, our formerly feral friend who had decided that she wouldn't tolerate this nonsense.

"If you can't get along like decent cats," she announced, "you're both suspended from cat choir. Is that understood?"

"But Clarice!" Harriet cried.

"No buts! Either you behave, or you're out. And that goes for you too, Shanille!"

"But Clarice!" Shanille lamented.

"Enough!" Clarice roared, causing both rivals to quickly shut up. "And now you're going to behave like grown-ups, and not like a couple of brats."

"Yes, Clarice," said both Shanille and Harriet in unison.

"And if I see one more cameraman in here, I'm going to attack," she added as she decided to direct her ire at the bright white lights and the bulky cameras. And since they obviously hadn't understood her threat, she decided to put her money where her mouth was and approached the camera crew in a threatening fashion that gave the two men pause. And when that still didn't do the trick, she bit the cameraman on the ankle.

"Hey, are you nuts!" said the guy.

Our fellow cat choir members seemed to enjoy the spectacle. So much so that they decided to join in the fun. And so the next moment saw a camera operator and a boom man race off as fast as their legs could carry them, after having sustained several bites on the ankles and other parts of their anatomy.

"Good riddance," said Clarice with satisfaction. "Now let's sing."

Unfortunately, before we could do that, suddenly big lights flashed on all sides, and as we shielded our eyes from the glare, sounds of cats in distress were everywhere around us.

"What's going on, Max?" Dooley yelled.

"I don't know, Dooley," I said. "Maybe it's the reality TV people? Back for another take?"

But before I knew what was happening, suddenly a rough hand grabbed me by the scruff of the neck and hoisted me into the air. Moments later, I was being thrown into a steel cage along with Dooley, Harriet, and Brutus, and the door was slammed shut. The cage was then lifted into the air and deposited onto a waiting truck.

"Max?" said Dooley.

"Huh?"

"I think we've been catnapped."

I sighed. "Not again."

CHAPTER 28

But he was correct. We had been catnapped. Which, I might mention for those of you who haven't been following my chronicles, has happened before. Only this time I had the impression that the operation was more professionally executed than the last time we were in this situation. The cages were of better quality, and so were the trucks. We'd gone from being abducted by a couple of amateur criminals to being snagged by professionals. The Michelin company would definitely have awarded these people five stars, and maybe even an extra star for effort. Before long, the truck was en route to a destination unknown, and I wondered where they were taking us and what their plans were.

"I just hope they won't turn us into sausages," said Dooley moodily.

"Maybe they want us to perform a special show?" said Harriet hopefully. "You know, like for some billionaire? These people must have heard of cat choir and decided to airlift us in for a special concert. Ooh, we could be singing for the President on the White House lawn next!"

"I very much doubt whether a lot of people have heard of cat choir," I said.

"Then maybe they've seen the show," said Harriet stubbornly, "and they want me to perform, with you guys as backing vocals."

"The show hasn't aired yet," I pointed out. "So nobody will have seen you, Harriet."

"I still think we're being brought to an undisclosed location for a special purpose," she said. "Famous stars like us don't just get kidnapped for…" She gasped. "Oh, my God! That's it!"

"What?" asked Brutus.

"We're stars now, you guys. And stars get kidnapped all the time! For ransom, you know, or because some madman out there wants to meet them."

"We should have hired bodyguards," Brutus said. "Stars have bodyguards, don't they? So now that we're stars, we should be awarded the same privilege. Then this wouldn't have happened."

"Clarice can be our bodyguard," said Dooley. "She did a pretty good job with those camera people."

But clearly, these abductors were no match for Clarice. Even though I could imagine she would have bitten quite a few of them in their ankles, at the end of the day, it's hard to fight superior numbers and the obvious professionalism these people brought to the job.

Before long, the truck jerked to a halt, and moments later, the doors were opened and our cage was dragged from the back of the truck. And as we were being carried, I couldn't see where we were going, unfortunately, as they had thrown a curtain over our cage.

"I wonder who it will be," said Harriet. "Leo DiCaprio, maybe, or the Prince of Brunei? I'll bet it's a very important person who's paid millions for a special concert of cat choir."

I rolled my eyes at this and decided to refrain from comment this time.

The cage was positioned on the floor, and for a moment, silence reigned. Then suddenly, a familiar voice reached my ear. It was Gran!

"What is this?" she asked.

"These are the cats you inherited," said another voice, male this time, and belonging, if I wasn't mistaken, to Sammie Paston.

"You brought three hundred cats into our home?!" Odelia's voice cried in dismay.

"Well… I didn't know where else to take them," said Sammie. "Since you haven't actually opened the zoo yet. So for now, you'll just have to keep them in here."

"God, this is the nightmare that keeps on giving," Chase said.

And then suddenly, the curtain was yanked off the cage, and Odelia cried, "But those are my cats!"

Sammie stared at us, then at the person who had yanked away the curtain, giving him a distinct look of disapproval. "You idiot!" he said. The guy looked like a mercenary, I decided: all muscle and shaved head and army fatigues.

"You ordered three hundred cats, you got three hundred cats," the guy said with a shrug. "Contract fulfilled. Now if you'll sign here," he added, and shoved a clipboard into Sammie's face, leaving the man no option but to sign.

"Why did you lock our cats up in these cages?" asked Gran.

"Look, it's Shanille," said Marge.

"Who?" asked Tex.

"Father Reilly's cat."

"And Kingman," said Gran.

"And Buster, Tom, Tigger, Misty, Shadow, Missy…" said Odelia.

The mercenary had left, and as I glanced around, I saw that dozens of cages stood stacked in our living room, hundreds of cats inside them. And if I wasn't mistaken, our family did not look very happy with this state of affairs.

"There must be some kind of mistake," Sammie said feebly. "I asked for your cousin Beatrice's cats to be transported here, but for some reason, they delivered these."

"Something very fishy is going on here," said Gran, giving the executor and wannabe reality show producer the evil eye. "What are you up to, buddy boy?"

"Nothing, I swear! I'm just as shocked as you are!"

"Let's get these out of here," said Marge as she started opening the cages. It took a while since there were dozens of them, but after a while, the living room was filled with cats, all complaining at the tops of their lungs at the fate that had befallen them. In the end, Marge, Odelia and Gran had no other recourse but to offer all of them a hearty meal to compensate for the ordeal they had been put through at the behest of Sammie Paston. And as I studied the guy, I was under the impression that he was suddenly suffering from an acute case of cold feet. For as our humans busied themselves with feeding hundreds of felines, offering them our food, the man was making desperate attempts to make himself scarce.

"Dooley, Harriet, Brutus," I said curtly. "Follow me."

And as they followed me, I followed Mr. Paston, who had skedaddled through the kitchen door and was now legging it around the house, then across the street and into the house belonging to Rebecca Wilkinson.

"Where is he going?" asked Harriet.

"I have no idea," I said. "But I'll bet he's up to no good."

Oddly enough, of the camera crews, there was not a single sign. As if they had all mysteriously disappeared after the ankle-biting incident at the park. Maybe as a species, they had decided that their environment had turned too hostile for their taste and had returned to reality show land to harass some other hapless people intent on becoming famous.

Before long, we were following Sammie up the stairs and then another flight of stairs until we found ourselves in a cramped attic room. And as we watched, the man was dumping stuff into large, bulky canvas bags. I saw a tripod on a camera, another one with a telescope, recording equipment, and generally the kind of stuff you'd typically see at a stakeout.

"Looks like he's been spying on us," said Brutus.

"Yeah, I think it's safe to say that Sammie hasn't been entirely honest with us," I agreed. And as I glanced down, my eye was suddenly drawn to a press pass lying on the floor. It featured Sammie's picture, only the name on the press pass was Kevin Thomson, and it said he worked for the *New York Chronicle*.

I pointed to the press pass. "I think this explains a lot."

They took a closer look at the press pass, and Brutus nodded. "Looks like our man Sammie is, in actual fact, an undercover reporter."

"I wonder what his angle is, though," said Harriet. "Why was he spying on us, and why the subterfuge?"

The guy had pressed his phone to his ear and was talking rapidly into the device. "I gotta bail, boss. Yeah, I think they're onto me. The gig is up. What?" He listened for a moment. "No, I'm not doing this story anymore. So what if they can talk to cats? I haven't managed to collect a single shred of evidence that what you're saying is true. They're just a regular family with a regular bunch of cats, though maybe a little more aggressive than most, so I'm pulling the plug." He was pacing the floor now, looking extremely agitated. "I'm not staying here one second longer. Didn't you hear what I said? They're onto me! I ordered three hundred cats, and you know what those idiots did? They kidnapped the Poole cats! Go figure! So the game is up, and I'm out of here before they come after me. Maybe I should have mentioned that they've got not one but two cops in the family, so if they find out that I've been spying on them so I can write a story about this so-called 'talking to cats' nonsense you've been going on about, there will be hell to pay, and I might never get out of Dodge!"

As he was talking, he had turned to face our direction, and when he caught sight of the four of us, he froze. Then he lowered the phone, tucked it away, and held up his hands in a gesture of defense. "Easy now, kitties," he said. "Let's not do anything rash now, you hear."

"I'm going for the ankles, Max," Brutus announced viciously.

"Oh, sugar biscuit, don't hurt yourself," said Harriet.

Suddenly, the man yelped in horror.

"See?" said Brutus with satisfaction. "He's scared of us already."

But when I glanced behind us, I saw that dozens of our cat choir colleagues had joined us in that small attic room, with more arriving every moment.

"When I saw you sneaking out, I decided to follow," said Clarice. "And I'm glad I did."

"Is this the guy who kidnapped us?" asked Kingman.

"This is him," I confirmed.

"He also spied on our family," said Harriet.

"He's a reporter," said Dooley. "And he wanted to find out if our humans can talk to us. And so he decided to invent this whole story about the inheritance, didn't he, Max?"

"That's right."

"So... no five million?" asked Harriet.

"No five million," I confirmed.

"And no zoo?" asked Brutus.

"No zoo."

"We're the zoo," Clarice growled.

"Easy now," said the guy, moving back until he reached the wall and could go no further. A look of panic had appeared in his eyes, and he definitely didn't look like a happy camper now. But before some of the more vengeful elements in cat choir could attack, a loud voice announced, "What's going on here!"

The voice belonged to Chase, who had decided to follow the sudden migration of cats across the street.

"Oh, Detective Kingsley," said Kevin Thomson. "I'm so glad to see you. These cats..." He swallowed. "They want to attack me!"

Next to Chase, Odelia had also appeared, and as we explained to her what was going on and drew her attention to the press pass, she picked it up off the floor and gave it to her husband.

"Kevin Thomson?" asked the latter. "Reporter for the *New York Chronicle*?"

The man nodded, sweat pouring down his brow. "That's right. My editor... he wanted me to do a story on your family. He had heard a rumor that you could talk to cats. Nonsense, of course. But nevertheless, he decided that maybe there was a story, and so he sent me down here for that purpose."

"So the inheritance, the five million, Cousin Beatrice?" asked Odelia.

"All lies," the reporter admitted. "There is no Cousin Beatrice or any inheritance. My editor thought it might induce you to play ball. And then we could film you and hopefully catch you in the act of communicating with your cats. But of course, we both know that's all horse manure. So if you could please let me leave now..."

"Buddy, you're not going anywhere," Chase grunted viciously.

"Yeah, you put us through the wringer," Odelia chimed in, "with your camera crews and your promises and by abducting our cats."

"That was a miscommunication," said the guy, wiping his brow nervously.

"There seem to have been a lot of those," Chase said.

Behind him, Marge and Tex had appeared, and also Gran, making the little attic room very crowded.

The guy, realizing he wasn't going to make a quick getaway, decided to surrender. "Okay, so please arrest me," he told Chase. "Before these cats skin me alive."

Chase nodded. "You got that right. You've made a lot of enemies in this town, Mr. Thomson. And now you're going to pay for your crimes."

"I know. Just go ahead and arrest me already. Take me to a nice cell in your police station. But please, whatever you do, don't leave me alone with these monsters!"

"Can I bite his ankle, Max?" asked Clarice. "Just a nibble?"

"I'm not sure that's a good idea," I told her.

"And besides, you already had plenty of ankle tonight," Harriet added with a grin.

We all laughed, and the guy looked even more scared than before. He didn't seem to be all that fond of cats. Which is odd for a guy who was prepared to make a reality show about us.

But then Chase finally seemed to feel sorry for him, so he arrested him and led him away. The sea of cats split like the Red Sea as we all directed angry looks at the guy, who made whimpering noises as he navigated the mob of angry felines. Before long, he was descending the stairs with Chase, to spend the night in the lockup. And I think he was glad about it.

The homeowner must have heard the noise and now

came shuffling up the stairs. "What's going on here?" asked Mrs. Wilkinson. "Are you harassing that nice Agent Cooper?"

"That nice Agent Cooper has been harassing us," Gran pointed out. "By abducting our cats, feeding us all kinds of lies, and generally behaving like a terrible human being."

"But he had to, Vesta," said Becca Wilkinson. "He's a G-man, you know, and even though I can certainly sympathize with some of your ideas, you can't just go around setting off nuclear bombs just because you don't like this or that person."

"What are you talking about?" asked Marge, thoroughly mystified.

"Well, Agent Cooper works for the FBI, you see, and he knows about that bomb you're building in your basement, Vesta. And so he was keeping an eye on you to make sure you didn't accidentally set it off in our neighborhood. But if you want to go ahead and set it off in Brooklyn, I'm sure that's fine. My sister-in-law lives there, you see, and I never liked her."

"But I'm not building a bomb in my basement!" Gran cried.

"Yeah, and Cooper isn't an FBI guy but a reporter," Tex added.

"He was sent here by the editor of the *Chronicle* to write an article about us," Odelia explained. "Only he told us a bunch of lies in the process, and also kidnapped our cats."

"Oh, dear," said Mrs. Wilkinson. "Is that a fact?"

"It is," Gran confirmed.

"So... you're not a terrorist?"

"No, I'm not."

Mrs. Wilkinson seemed disappointed by this. "Oh, well. I guess you can't have it all."

CHAPTER 29

Compared to the stirring events as they had unfolded, we spent a peaceful night at home. Or at least we would have, if not suddenly around two o'clock in the morning, I was suddenly awakened by a strange sound at our bedroom door. Dooley and I like to sleep at the foot of the bed, you see, and so when I woke up and saw a tiny light moving in the air nearby, for a moment I thought it might be a firefly. But then I suddenly felt a soft object touch my head, and I jumped up with a loud screech, figuring I was being attacked again.

Immediately, the light in the room was turned on, and both Odelia and Chase sat up in bed. Before us, a cameraman stood looking at us with a sheepish look on his face, accompanied by a boom man who must have accidentally lowered his boom mic too low, causing it to thump my head.

"Howdy, folks," said the cameraman. "We didn't want to wake you up, so if you could go right back to sleep, that would be great."

"I think you better get out of here," said Chase in an

implacable voice. "Before I arrest you and throw both your asses in the slammer."

"But, sir," said the boom man, "there's no need to take that tone."

"Yeah, you signed a contract," the cameraman reminded us.

"That contract is null and void since the party of the second part is in jail," Chase said.

The two men shared a look of surprise. "You arrested Kev—Sammie?"

"You don't have to pretend anymore," said Odelia, adopting a kinder tone than her husband. "We know all about Mr. Thomson's assignment to write a story about us and pretending to make a reality show. So you can both go home now. The job is done."

"But... we'll still get paid, right?" asked the guy.

"You'll have to talk to the editor at the *Chronicle* for that," she said.

"And now get out," said Chase. "Before I throw you out."

"Of course, detective," said the cameraman. "Right away, detective."

"Can I just say that you make a lovely couple?" said the boom man. "The way you guys snuggle when you sleep. So cute."

"Out!" Chase yelled.

And out they went.

Things returned to normal after that, or at least as normal as they ever get in Hampton Cove. At least no cats were being kidnapped or members of our family followed around and filmed in their beds by a camera crew.

"Max?"

"Yes, Dooley," I said.

"So about that five million."

"There is no five million, Dooley."

"Oh."

He was quiet for a moment, then: "So about that zoo."

"There is no zoo."

"Oh."

Odelia stirred. "Can we please all go to sleep now?" she asked in a sleepy voice.

"Yes, can we please go to sleep now?" echoed Grace, who sleeps in a cot next to her parents.

And so we did as we were told and promptly fell asleep. Though I have to say a part of me was still on high alert, just in case more nocturnal marauders showed up. Luckily for us —and them—no one did.

It was a good thing that we had all decided to take advantage of the peace and quiet to have a good night's rest, for the next day promised to be filled with plenty of activity. At the breakfast table, Odelia outlined the itinerary for the day, and it listed quite a number of interviews. Or, in fact, you could probably describe them as re-interviews, as we had to talk to some people a second time since apparently they hadn't told us the truth the first time. Among those on Odelia and Chase's list were Liam Cass, Stella Cass, and also Melanie Bell. And if that wasn't enough, we also had to go talk to the people who ran the outdoor center located on the shore of Lake Mario.

"So those people who kept following us around," said Grace as our humans enjoyed a hearty breakfast. "They won't be back?"

"No, they won't be back," I confirmed.

"Oh, too bad," said the toddler. "I kinda like having them around, you know."

"You like being filmed?" I asked.

PURRFECT ZOO

"Well, maybe not being filmed, exactly, but I like a house full of people, and they certainly brought life to our home."

"That, they certainly did," I said as I remembered that duo from last night, observing how we slept and filming everything.

"And also," she said, "I was looking forward to living in a zoo. I like zoos. Goats and sheep and giraffes and elephants. I think it must be fun to own your own zoo."

"This particular zoo only had cats in it," I reminded her. Which should have raised all kinds of alarm bells when Kevin Thomson had first suggested the idea to us, as there are probably no zoos anywhere in the world that only house cats. Cats don't like spending time in a glass cage being gaped at, you see. And so they would have tried to escape the first chance they got. You would start out with a zoo of three hundred, and only a couple of days later, you'd end up with nothing.

"Okay, so are you going to solve that murder today, Max?" asked Grace as she put a piece of apple into her mouth and bit down.

"I'm not sure," I said. "So far, we haven't collected all the information we need yet. There is still a lot of stuff we don't know about what happened yesterday and the night before at the lake. So until we do, it's hard to figure out what exactly went down."

"I'm sure you'll figure it out eventually," said Grace, showing a confidence in my powers of deduction that I didn't share, to be honest. I had a feeling that I'd already been offered the deciding clue, but somehow I simply couldn't put it all together.

Chase finished first, as usual, with Odelia a close second, and Grace coming in last. And so we all got into the car, and after we had dropped off Grace at daycare, wishing her a great day, we headed back to Cass Motors to talk some more with some of the main principals in the Fisher murder case. We saw Liam first, and this time Chase put it to him straight.

"We have it on good authority that you were moving to Texas, Liam. So what can you tell us about that?"

He gave us a look of surprise, but then quickly admitted that the story was true. "Allie and I decided it together. She wanted to get away from her mom and dad, and I wanted to get away from mine, so it was a no-brainer. And then when she was accepted at the University of Texas, we were both over the moon, you know? I applied for a job at one of the bigger Ford dealerships in Austin, and they said I was welcome to join their team any time. And so all that was left was telling our parents, which we were planning to do when we got closer to the date."

"But why didn't you want to stay here?"

"Because I want to be my own man, you know? Out here I'll always be my dad's son, with him making all the decisions, whereas out there I'd be standing on my own two feet, capable of making my own decisions. It's not that I don't love my dad, but you can't understand what it's been like living in his shadow for all these years. Don't get me wrong, I've learned a ton, but he's so... overbearing. I feel as if I don't get any air. And so we both decided that since we wanted to be together, and Allie needed to get away, we would move there together. She would study, I would work, and we'd try to build a life there."

"Were you planning to return at some point after Allie had graduated, or did you plan to stay out there permanently?" asked Odelia.

"Permanently," said Liam with a nod. "Allie had the strongest motivation to move away, of course, but I was happy to be away from here too. And out there, nobody would know us, and we could simply start over, which gave us both such a sense of freedom. We couldn't wait to leave."

He gave us a sad look. "Only now it turns out we waited too long."

"Your dad..."

"Yes?"

"According to your mom, he was home with her the night Allie died. But you didn't see him, did you?"

He thought for a moment, then shook his head. "No, I didn't see him, which doesn't mean he wasn't home," he hastened to add.

"There's something else," said Chase. "We talked to Melissa Bell, Allison's friend, and she told us a completely different story. She said that Allison was breaking up with you, that she couldn't stand that you were so needy and clingy."

"She said that?"

Chase nodded. "She also claimed that the reason Allison was moving to Texas was to get away from you."

"God, she's a real piece of work, that one, isn't she? There's simply nothing about that that's even remotely true. You can ask this person," he said, taking out his phone. "We already arranged to rent an apartment in Austin. This is the number for the owner. She'll confirm it."

"So Allison wasn't staying with Melissa's aunt?"

Liam frowned. "Melissa has an aunt in Austin? That's news to me." He hesitated.

"Yes?"

"Well, the thing is... before Allison and I got together, Melissa and I dated briefly. It was a summer fling, and when I met Allie, I got together with her. But I always got the impression that Melissa was unhappy about that, even though she never said. It's possible that she's making up this stuff to make me look bad, you know. To make you guys think that I hurt Allie. But I didn't, I swear. I was in my room that night, and I never left again."

"You gave us the impression that you weren't happy that Allison paid a visit to Melissa instead of spending more time with you, though."

"Yeah, I know. I didn't like her hanging out with Melissa all the time. I had a feeling Melissa was trying to poison Allie's mind against me. Not that she would have succeeded. Our connection was too strong for that, but still. It didn't feel right to me that she would spend so much time with her."

"You also told us that you were upset with Allison for going off to college and leaving you behind."

He gave a shrug. "I didn't want you to know that Allie and I had other plans. Now that she's gone, I didn't see a reason for my parents to know we were planning to move to Austin."

"Those plans are off?"

"They're off," he said with a sigh. "Now that Allie is gone, there's no point in me going out there. And even though my dad can be difficult as a boss, I'm sure I'll manage. And besides, in a couple of years, he'll probably retire, and then Cass Motors will be mine to run. Though without Allie, it just won't be the same."

CHAPTER 30

Next, we found ourselves back in Liam's dad's office, with the big guy hemming and hawing when Odelia and Chase asked him straight out where he had been the night that Allison Fisher was murdered, for they were quite sure that he hadn't been at home watching the *Masked Singer* with his wife as he had claimed. It took him a while to come to the conclusion that he wasn't served by continuing to lie to us and finally decided to come clean.

But before he did, he closed the door to his office.

"Okay, so you're right," he said. "I wasn't at home watching TV with my wife. I was right here in this office."

"You were here at midnight?"

He nodded. "I'm a workaholic, all right? My wife hates it, and she keeps telling me I should relax and smell the roses and let someone else take over. But I just can't. I've built this business from scratch and it's taken me years to get where I am now, and I just have this feeling that if I don't give it my all, things will collapse around me and the business will fail, and we'll be poor again. Just like we were before. So it's very hard for me to let go, which is why I spend most weeknights in my office until well past one o'clock or two o'clock or three. Sometimes I even sleep in this chair and wake up when Stella comes in at six."

"So why didn't you tell us?" asked Chase.

"Because I don't have an alibi! So I asked Stella to tell you that I was home with her, and even though she hates lying to the police, she would hate it a lot more if I was arrested for murder and Cass Motors would sink like a stone. You see, before we started this business together, Stella and I, we were both poor as church mice, and so we both have a very strong incentive to keep going and never to return to what life was like before."

"I understand, Mr. Cass, but you still should have told us," said Chase. "Lying to the police is never the answer. If anything, it makes you look bad, and so now we have no choice but to put you on our list of suspects."

"But why would I want to kill Allie, huh? I could see how good she and Liam were together. I loved that kid like my own daughter!"

"Because you were afraid that Allison might convince your son to leave Cass Motors?" Odelia suggested.

For a moment, the garage owner didn't speak, then he finally nodded. "I know that Liam was thinking about moving to Austin. I know he doesn't know that we know, but we do. The dealership he applied to in Austin contacted me for a reference, which is how we found out what he and Allie were up to. So did that make me disappointed? Of course it did. I was training him to take over at some point. But was I prepared to murder Allie for that reason? Absolutely not." He sat a little straighter. "Like I said, Stella and I loved that girl like our own daughter. And I would never, ever have hurt a hair on her head. Ever!"

* * *

MELISSA BELL WAS A TOUGHER NUT to crack. When we paid a visit to her school, the principal had her brought from the classroom to the principal's office so we could talk to the girl in private. But when Chase put it to her that she had lied about her friend's relationship with Liam, at first she denied it.

"No, it was exactly as I told you: Allie couldn't wait to get away from Liam. She was afraid of him. Afraid he would hurt her if he found out she was leaving for Texas."

"Melissa," said Odelia gently, "we know that you don't have an aunt in Austin. We talked to your parents, and they told us as much, and we saw the rental agreement Liam and Allie had signed. They were moving out there together, and Liam had already secured a job at a Ford dealership out there, and Allie was going to study while he worked to support both of them. So why don't you tell us the truth? And tell us why you lied?"

At this point, the girl finally broke down, and it took quite a number of tissues before she managed to stem the flood. "I'm in love with him, all right? I've been in love with Liam long before Allie ever entered the scene, but the moment she did, it was almost as if I didn't exist anymore. She completely turned his head and he dumped me like yesterday's news, as if I didn't mean anything. It was very hard to stay friends with her after that, but I like to think of myself as not a spiteful person, and so I swore I'd get over it. Only it was so hard to see him all the time. And especially to see the two of them together. Smiling, happy and in love when, by all rights, he should have been mine. Mine!" she cried, thumping her chest as she said it, her eyes shooting fire. But then she broke down into sniffles again. "Look, I know what you're thinking. That I was so jealous of Allie I followed her that night and killed her. But I didn't, I swear. I could never do anything like that, no matter how upset I was with her. And besides, we patched things up. That's the reason she paid me a visit that night. She had heard from Liam that I was behaving strangely, and so she wanted to talk to me about it. Especially since she would be leaving soon, and she didn't want there to be bad blood between us. So we talked, and I finally decided to forgive her and move on. We hugged, and she left. And that's the last time I saw her."

"So how are we to know that this time you're telling us the truth?" asked Chase.

"Because I am!"

"Even though you have just admitted to having a perfect motive for murdering Allison?"

"I didn't do it," she repeated. "I just didn't, you have to believe me."

"I'm inclined to believe her, Max," said Dooley.

"Yeah, me too," I said.

"She seems like a nice girl, and nice girls don't murder other nice girls."

I smiled. "Nice girls can become very upset when their friends steal their boyfriends away from them," I pointed out. "And so Melissa certainly had a good reason to get rid of her friend. That's why she may have been hoping to get back together with Liam."

"Do you think she will? Get back together with Liam?"

"It's possible," I allowed.

Chase and Odelia asked the girl a couple of follow-up questions, trying to trap her in another lie, but apparently, she was done telling lies. She also admitted that Allison had indeed been afraid of the lake, and would have hated going swimming out there. I had to say I agreed with my friend. If Melissa was the killer, she certainly deserved a prize for best actress, for she seemed truly devastated by the death of her friend.

* * *

Dooley and I sat on the lakeshore while our humans pottered about. According to their investigation, this was the exact spot where Allison had gone into the lake two nights ago, before her body had been swept away by the current and had eventually ended up being snagged by the fishing line of poor Cameron Brooks, giving the pensioner the fright of his life.

"If only these shrubs could talk, Max," said Dooley, referring to the shrubs that lined the shoreline at this point. The spot had already been thoroughly combed for clues, including possible signs of a struggle, but unfortunately, nothing had been found that pointed to the identity of Allison's killer, or even if there had actually been a struggle. It was still a distant possibility that the girl had been fed up with life and had decided to end things herself. Though if the story of her and Liam having already secured an apartment in Austin was true, and according to Chase it was, that was starting to look more and more unlikely.

No, in my mind, there was not a shred of doubt that Allison, like her parents, had been the victim of murder. From the point where we now sat staring out across the lake, which was calm and peaceful at that moment, it was only a couple of hundred yards to the outdoor center where potential witnesses could have seen or heard something. But according to the police officers who had interviewed everyone present, no one had noticed anything out of the ordinary that night. But since Chase and Odelia are nothing if not meticulous, they decided to head over there and ask the owner if he hadn't recalled anything in the time that had passed.

When we arrived there, the place was quiet. We could see a class of young children in sailing boats on the lake, being taught their first lessons in learning how to navigate their crafts. But inside the bar, only one person sat nursing a hot chocolate and reading his paper. Behind the bar, we found the owner of the outdoor center, a bronzed man with graying hair who looked as if he enjoyed spending his leisure time on a boat on the lake.

Chase produced his badge, and so did Odelia, and the guy offered to take a seat at a nearby table so they could talk in peace. His name was Mark Thomas, and he had been operating the outdoor center for twenty years now, catering to tourists, locals, but also schools, like the kids that were out on the water now.

"No, I have to say I haven't remembered anything out of the ordinary," he said. "And believe me, I've racked my brain trying to recollect. It's such a tragic story, that poor girl dying not three hundred yards from where we were having a party, which is probably the reason why nobody noticed. She could have screamed her head off, and because of the loud music, nobody would have heard a thing."

"You never saw her in here on that night or any previous night?"

"No, I'm afraid I didn't. Though it's possible she came in here, of course. Our bar is pretty popular, and not just with our regular clientele. People enjoy coming out here on a summer night to sit by the lake. We also host bigger groups like wedding parties, birthday parties, and all of that. It's a pretty lively place, not just on the weekends, though we get more people on Friday nights and Saturday nights than usual, of course. Sundays are also pretty busy."

"Well, thank you for your time, Mr. Thomas," said Chase, getting up.

But Mark Thomas wasn't done yet. "Like I said, I've been thinking a lot about that poor kid, and of course, I've heard the stories about her parents not being the best parents a kid could hope for. In fact, I had a couple in here who said that Allison was thinking about running away from home since things were pretty bad between herself and her folks. Is it possible she took a boat out to the other side? The lake stretches all the way to Hampton Keys, and there are a lot of campsites out there, some of them catering to tourists, but some have permanent residents who stay there winter and summer. So maybe she was thinking about heading out there and hiding out from her parents? And maybe she got into trouble on the lake, and her boat took on water? It's happened before, you know, even to the most experienced sailor. There are currents in the middle of the lake that can get pretty treacherous when you don't know how to handle yourself and your vessel. It's possible she was surprised by them and got in trouble, and of course, out there, nobody will hear you scream."

CHAPTER 31

Uncle Alec had organized another meeting in his office, only this time the mood wasn't as upbeat as last time when Odelia and Chase were still full of hope to crack this case soon. Now, after all the evidence they had collected and the witness statements, they seemed even further away from finding the answer than before.

"Okay, so let's go over our possible suspects one by one," the Chief offered. "First, the theory that Mike tried to kill his wife, only she survived the attack long enough to attack him."

"I'm sorry, but I don't buy that," said Chase. "Nobody could have survived that knife wound, and certainly not long enough to chase after Mike and attack him in that garden house. And besides, we found Mike's blood in Chloe's wound, so that proves that Chloe was killed *after* Mike was stabbed, and not before."

"Okay, fine," said the Chief. "I happen to agree with you. So let's reduce that to the realm of fairy tales. Next, we have Suzette Peters. The theory here being that she was secretly in love with Mike, so she killed the guy's wife to get rid of her and have Mike for herself. But then why would she also kill Mike?"

"Because he rejected her?" Odelia suggested.

The Chief grimaced. "Seems a little far-fetched to me. Also, the Uber driver's records confirm that Miss Peters arrived at the scene at ten o'clock, so that seems to rule her out. Unless she was a fast worker and managed to murder two people in the time it took my mother and your cats to arrive there. No, I think we can safely scratch her as a suspect. Which brings us to Mike's boss, Bruno McIntyre. He was nervous about Mike's arguments with his wife casting the business in a negative light, potentially losing them customers but also staff members. There was a big brouhaha at their last work party, with Chloe creating a big scene, and no business owner likes that kind of thing."

"He claims he was at the office, and we've got witness statements from several of his colleagues who corroborate this," said Chase. "So unless he managed to sneak out unseen, drive over to the Fishers, murder both Mike and his wife, and sneak back, I don't think he's our man."

"Let's put him on the list of possibles," Uncle Alec said as he put a checkmark next to Mr. McIntyre's name. "I like him for this, you know. He's got a ruthless quality that makes me wonder if he couldn't have done this."

"Next is Liam Cass," said Chase. "Liam was in love with Allison and was pretty upset at the way her parents were treating her, especially her mom. So is it inconceivable that he decided to do something about it?"

The Chief leaned back in his chair and directed his gaze at the ceiling. "Okay, so let's suppose for one moment that this..." He consulted his notes. "... Mark Thomas, the guy who runs the outdoor center, is right, and that Allison and Liam decided to get her out of the house because things between the girl and her mom had escalated, and for her own safety, she couldn't stay there one minute longer. So they decided to meet by the lake and take a boat across to Hampton Keys, where Allison could stay in one of the empty caravans until they left for Texas. Only they got into trouble halfway through the crossing, and the boat sank. Liam made it back alive, but Allison didn't. Racked with grief, but also extremely upset with Allison's parents, who he blamed for the death of his girlfriend, he swam back to shore, vowing revenge. Which he got the next morning when he murdered the Fishers." He held up a finger. "We know he wasn't seen by his mom after ten o'clock, so he could easily have snuck back out of the house, either through the window or the back door, and then back in later."

"He was at the garage at ten o'clock in the morning," said Odelia. "Though it's true that he could probably have snuck out there as well and returned after committing both murders."

"It's a possibility," Chase allowed, "but we don't have any witnesses and no evidence that puts him at the crime scene."

The Chief sighed. "I'm putting him at the top of my list because, well, motive. Next, we have... Carroll and Stella Cass?"

"Liam was leaving for Texas, and the Casses weren't happy about it," Chase explained. "Which makes me think they could have decided to kill Allison so Liam would stay in Hampton Cove."

"But then why also kill her parents?"

Odelia thought for a moment. "Carroll claims they loved Allison like a daughter, so it's also possible that after learning of Allison's death from Liam, they decided to take care of the girl's parents, blaming them for what happened to Allison."

"But they were both at Cass Motors," said the Chief. "Though, of course, either of them could have snuck out and done the deed, then got back."

"And finally, we also have Melissa Bell," said Chase. "Who admits that she's in love with Liam and very upset with Allison for stealing him away from her. So she could have been involved in the death of her friend."

"But then why would she kill the Fishers?"

"We don't know if those murders are even connected, Chief," said Chase. "It's possible that Allison was killed by Melissa, and that her parents were killed by someone else entirely. Someone like Carroll or Liam Cass, or Bruno McIntyre, or Suzette Peters."

The Chief nodded as he frowned at his notes. "Kimberly Ross? How did she get on the suspect list?"

"Kimberly Ross is a member of the Pet Owners Society," said Odelia. "A self-declared dog nut, though according to the husband mostly the pedigreed kind. So if she heard that the Fishers were mistreating their dog, she may have snapped and decided to do something about it."

The Chief didn't look convinced. "A double homicide because someone mistreated their dog? Do you have any evidence for this?"

Both Chase and Odelia shook their heads. "None," Chase admitted.

"Then let's reduce this particular theory to the realm of fantasy," said the Chief and scratched out Kimberly Ross's name with a vigorous motion of his pen. "Which leaves us with... not all that much to go on," he said sadly. "An abundance of suspects but no evidence."

"Which is exactly why we called this meeting," said Chase. "We're stuck, Chief."

"Well, I'll say. So what do you propose to get unstuck?"

"I'm not sure. Re-interview all of the suspects a third time?"

"Did you talk to the neighbors?"

"We did. Nobody noticed anything."

"No screams, no suspicious characters hanging around? Cars?"

"Nothing."

For a moment, they were all silent, then the Chief suddenly looked down at us for some reason, and for what was probably the first time in history, grumbled, "You wouldn't have any idea, would you, Max?"

"Um..."

Odelia shook her head, causing her uncle to lightly curse. "When even Max doesn't have a clue, we're in deep doo-doo, people!"

CHAPTER 32

After the big meeting was over, Dooley and I decided to go for a walk. Odelia had impressed upon me the urgent need to try to work out what could have happened, and I had promised her to give it my best shot. We soon found ourselves drifting into Kingman's ken. The large cat seemed to have survived last night's ordeal pretty well, for he was shooting the breeze with two female felines and clearly feeling in his element. When we approached, the females wandered off, and Kingman gave us a slightly reproachful look.

"Now why did you have to go and do that, you guys!"

"Do what?" I asked.

"Chase those kitties away?"

"We didn't chase anyone away."

"Oh, but you did. When they saw the big Max arrive, they decided to shift. So why is that, you ask?"

"I didn't ask, but okay. Why is that?"

"Because of your reputation, Max!"

"And what is my reputation, exactly?" I asked, intrigued.

"You're a brainiac. A mental magician. You can run rings

around anyone with that razor-sharp mind of yours, and I don't know if you've ever realized this, but not everybody likes being run rings around, Max, especially those two girls that just left. One of them even told me that you once approached her and told her that within the next ten days she would develop a rash on her visage. And lo and behold, she did develop a rash, and let me tell you that she wasn't happy about it."

"I honestly don't remember," I admitted.

"Well, she does. And so she doesn't want to get another rash, which is why the moment she saw you homing in, she made herself scarce."

"But that's a logical fallacy, Kingman," I pointed out. "I'm not the one who caused the rash. I'm merely the one who pointed it out to her."

"Be that as it may, she didn't want to be seen with you, afraid you'll give her another rash."

"How did you do that, Max?" asked Dooley. "How did you predict that she was going to get a rash on her face?"

I thought hard, digging deep to recollect, but try as I might, this particular incident didn't rise to the surface.

"She told me that you said she had been in contact with a particular plant. English Ivy is what you called it."

"Oh, right!" I said. "Now I remember. Well, she had a piece of English Ivy leaf still attached to her person, which is why I told her she shouldn't go near that plant again, and I removed the leaf, hoping it wouldn't affect her."

"Well, it did, and now she associates you with the rash."

"Which doesn't make any sense at all."

"A word of advice, Max, next time when you see a female walking around with a piece of plant on her person, don't say anything. Just leave her be."

"But I can't do that!"

"I'm just telling you."

"Do I have a piece of leaf on me, Max?" asked Dooley.

I checked him over quickly and assured him that he was free of any leaves of a suspicious or rash-inducing nature.

"Oh, phew," said my friend. "And I just want you to know that if you ever see a leaf on me, you can tell me any time, Max, and I won't hold it against you."

"That's good to know, Dooley. Thank you."

Kingman grinned. "Oh, there was something I wanted to say to you, Max, but now it seems to have escaped me for some reason." He thought for a moment, but finally shook his head. "It will come to me."

We watched as Shanille walked up to us, followed by Harriet and Brutus. Almost like a gathering of cat choir on a smaller scale. And when Clarice also joined us, the gang was complete.

"I still have the taste of that guy's ankles in my mouth," Clarice revealed as she smacked her lips. "Tasted like... fish."

"How can a person's ankles taste like fish, Clarice?" asked Dooley with a laugh.

"Well, I'm telling you that guy's ankles tasted of fish."

"Maybe he had been eating a lot of fish?" Shanille suggested.

Between herself and Harriet hung a sort of embarrassed silence, I noticed, which wasn't surprising after the fracas they had been involved in last night. But since I hate these strained atmospheres, I finally decided to do something about it, so I said, "Shanille, Harriet has told me that she feels very ashamed about what happened last night, and she would like to apologize."

"No, I don't," said Harriet, looking very much surprised.

"In fact, she feels so ashamed she can't even admit it to you, but rest assured that she does. Feel very much ashamed, I mean."

"But I don't feel ashamed!" said Harriet.

"Oh, Harriet, it's all right," said Shanille. "I was also feeling embarrassed by my reaction."

"You were?"

"Absolutely. I should never have claimed that I'm the only important person in cat choir. All members are equally important, but the lead soprano is just that little bit more important than most."

"Well, that's good to hear," said Harriet, giving me a curious look.

"In fact, I couldn't do what I do without you, and that's the God's honest truth. So I wanted to apologize to you as well."

"Okay, fine," said Harriet with a shrug.

Shanille waited for a beat, then frowned. "So aren't you going to apologize to me?"

"Why should I? You just told me yourself that you were wrong and I was right."

"But I was also right in a sense. The conductor is the most important person in any choir."

"No, she's not."

"Oh, but she is."

"Without us, there wouldn't be a choir."

"Without me, there also wouldn't be a choir."

For a moment, the two cats stood face to face, then Clarice decided to step in once more. "Okay, you two, break it up. Now why is it that every time we're together, you got me playing policewoman? Can't you simply get along?" She pointed to Shanille. "You're important to cat choir." Then she pointed to Harriet. "And you're important. And I'm important, and so is Max, and so is Dooley. We're all important. This is not a competition or a popularity contest. Cat choir is a community, and all of its members are of equal importance. So just kiss already and make up, all right, because if you don't, I'm going to bang some heads together."

The prospect of having their heads banged together mustn't have appealed to either Shanille or Harriet, for they quickly kissed and made up. Okay, so maybe the kissing part didn't actually materialize, but they did promise Clarice to behave from now on, and I was glad of the reprieve.

"So have you found this dog Bella yet?" asked Shanille.

I shook my head. "No, I haven't. Though not for lack of trying, I can assure you."

"It's the dogs," said Kingman. "They all bond together. They've got this thing, this code of silence, you know. Omertà, the Italians call it. It's a mafia thing. That's what I wanted to tell you, Max, that I'm more convinced than ever that the Fishers were killed by the mob." And since I found myself staring at him in dismay, he continued, "You see, Mike Fisher flubbed a job. It happens, but in his case, since his client was a well-known mobster, he paid for it with his life. Max, where are you going? Max! Come back here!"

But I was already going, and going fast!

CHAPTER 33

Dooley, who had decided to follow his friend when he made his escape, caught up with Max halfway down the street. "What's wrong, Max?" he asked. "Why did you run away like that? Is it your tummy? Did you eat something that didn't agree with you? Or is it something Kingman said?"

Max gave him a sort of feverish look. "Exactly that," he said.

"Something Kingman said? But what?"

"Let's first see if my hunch plays out," said Max.

Dooley smiled to himself. Max always had these hunches, and more often than not, they did play out, and then Max often hit upon something brilliant. He hoped that his friend would hit on something brilliant now because they could definitely use it. Chase and Odelia seemed to be all out of ideas on how to solve this case, and if anyone could crack it, it was Max.

"So where are we going?" he asked.

"The Fishers," Max said curtly, and Dooley knew better

than to ask a lot of questions, for when Max had a bee in his bonnet, he should just let him follow it through to the end.

Before long, they had arrived in the neighborhood where the Fishers lived, and Dooley saw to his surprise that Max wasn't going to the Fishers' house but to that of their neighbor, Mrs. Malt. Edwina Malt was nowhere in sight, but that didn't seem to bother Max, for he set paw straight for the garden house at the back of the garden, and before long, stood before it, looking at it in a sort of intent fashion.

"What's wrong, Max?" asked Dooley. "What are we doing here?"

But Max put his paw to his lips and shook his head, indicating that Dooley should keep quiet. And then Max did the strangest thing: he put his ear to the door and listened intently. After a few moments, a smile appeared on his furry face, and Dooley could see that his eyes were flickering with the light of intelligence. Max's brainwave had panned out. He had hit the jackpot. And somehow Dooley knew just what they'd find behind that door.

"Bella, you can come out now," Max said. "It's all right. I know who killed your humans."

For a moment, there was no movement, but then suddenly the door swung open, and before them stood Bella, the Bichon Frisé who had formerly belonged to the Fishers and now, apparently, had found refuge in Edwina Malt's backyard.

"So who did it?" asked Bella. And when Max gave her the name, she nodded. "I didn't think you'd figure it out, Max. I really didn't."

Dooley smiled and said, "Max always figures it out, Bella."

* * *

Marcus Miller looked up at the gutter of his suburban home and wondered whether he should paint it himself or hire a professional. He could hire someone, of course, but that would cost money, and if he did it himself, they could use the funds for a nice vacation instead. Decisions, decisions.

Too bad Mike Fisher wasn't around anymore to ask if he could borrow his ladder. Though now that he thought of it... Mike was dead, but his ladder was still there, probably in the same spot it had been before: hanging on those hooks behind his garden house. So what if he went there to borrow it? Who would know? And who would mind? Mike sure as heck wouldn't. And what if he kept it? That was one fine ladder, and Mike, being the only one in their neighborhood who had such a fine ladder, had made himself real popular. Well, until they had all discovered the truth about the guy, of course.

He looked up when Edwina approached. "So I was thinking about borrowing Mike's ladder, Edwina," he said. "I'm sure he won't mind." He gave her a knowing look.

"No, I don't think he would," Edwina agreed. "Melanie not home?"

"She's inside. Why? Do you need her?"

"I need to talk to her, yeah."

"Mel!" he shouted.

Moments later, his wife walked out of the house, drying her hands on a dish towel. She joined him in looking up at that gutter. The paint had been peeling for a while now, and it was high time they did something about it.

"So what do you think, Mel? Do it myself or hire a pro?"

Mel made a face. She was even more cost-conscious than her husband. "I'll give you a hand if you like. Or we could even ask my brother to help out a couple of weekends in a row. We might even be able to replace those shingles over there that have gotten loose." She turned to Edwina. "Is there something you wanted to talk to me about?"

"Yeah, there is," Edwina admitted. But then another neighbor casually strode up. This was Chris Foster from down the road. With her blue hair fashionably tousled and her jeans coveralls, she looked as if she'd just walked off the pages of a fashion magazine, Marcus thought. But then she had always been the most zeitgeist-conscious of all of their neighbors. She did something in art, Marcus knew. Freelance photographer or art designer.

"You wanted to talk to me, Edwina?" asked Chris.

"Yeah, actually I wanted to talk to all of you," Edwina now said, causing Marcus to experience a ripple of concern.

"What's this about?" he asked as he redirected his attention from his gutter to their elderly next-door neighbor.

"Mike and Chloe," Edwina said quietly. "I think we should come clean."

The little ripple now turned into a roaring river of apprehension. "No way," he said. "We agreed we would never mention what happened again."

"I know we did," said Edwina. "But unfortunately, the police found out. They know, Marcus. They know what we did, and they came to me about it and told me I had a choice. Either confess to what happened, or..." She swallowed.

"Or?" Marcus prompted.

"Or they were going to make life really difficult for all of us."

"They're bluffing," said Mel. "They couldn't possibly know."

"Well, they do. They came to the house and laid it all out to me, in detail. I don't know how they know, but they know everything. What the Fishers did, what we did..." She gave them a miserable look. "It's over. We're done for."

"No, we're not!" said Marcus viciously. He'd worked too hard to create a dream life in the suburbs, and he wasn't going to give it up simply because some old woman lost her nerve. He stabbed an accusing finger at her. "You must have blabbed, didn't you? You told them."

"I didn't tell them anything! They have a source. They didn't tell me what source, but it must have been someone who was there because everything they told me could only have come from someone who knows exactly what we all did."

Marcus's eyes snapped to Chris, who held up her hands. "Hey, it wasn't me. I didn't tell them anything."

"So who was it?" He glanced at his wife, who gave him a frown.

"You're not seriously suggesting I talked to the cops, are you?"

"I don't understand," he said. Then suddenly, a thought occurred to him. Only last night, he'd been chatting with that new couple, the Rosses. And Robert Ross had told him that there was this rumor that Odelia Kingsley and her family could talk to their pets. Surely it wasn't possible that... But then he discarded the idea as quickly as it had reared its head. Of course not. That was simply crazy talk. Pets couldn't talk. Pets couldn't even think. They were walking pieces of meat, just like any other animal out there. Roast fillet on legs. Only humans had consciousness and a mind that could think and react and plot and plan...

A dog now came trotting up. It was that infuriating little yapper that used to belong to the Fishers but had now been adopted by Edwina. It was one of those ridiculous dogs that looked like a sausage. He would have given it a kick, but with Edwina standing next to him, that was not advisable. The dog just stood there, wagging its tongue and giving them all a blank look. He now remembered the dog had been there on the day that they had... Well, that didn't mean anything. Dogs were dumb creatures. Bella couldn't possibly have told what she saw to those detectives that kept giving them grief, asking a million questions.

"We should tell them," Edwina now repeated. "They know, and they've suggested a deal. If we confess to what we did, they'll take extenuating circumstances into account. If we don't, they'll throw the book at us."

Marcus saw that the old lady was scared. Clearly, they had done a real number on her, trying to intimidate her into a confession. But that wouldn't work with him. He would never confess, whatever they brought to bear on him.

"These are scare tactics," he told the others. "They're bluffing. They've got nothing, and now they're simply trying to bully us into a confession. If we stay strong, there's absolutely nothing they can do, apart from this little fishing expedition, which is going to get them nowhere. If we stick to the story."

But he had the impression the others were already buckling under the pressure. Edwina looked as if she was on the verge of bursting into tears, Mel was biting her lip and giving him pleading glances, and even Chris Foster seemed about to crack.

"We promised!" he said. "We made a deal!"

"We did something very wrong, Marcus," Mel said. "We took a life. Two lives, even. We should never have done it."

"I should never have listened to you," said Chris, suddenly rounding on him. "We should have gone to the cops, just like I said. But instead, you came up with this crazy idea that we should take the law into our own hands. And now look where we are. Soon, we'll all be in prison! Our lives are over!"

"Our lives are not over," he promised them. "If we simply

stay the course, there's absolutely nothing they can do. And besides, they were never going to hold Mike and Chloe accountable for what they did to their daughter. They killed her and then tried to cover it up!"

"We still should have told the police," Chris insisted. "Now we're the ones who will have to stand trial instead of the Fishers. It's all going to be about us, not about the real culprits in this whole sordid affair."

He thought for a moment. Clearly, his neighbors were ready to blab. And they were adamant to drag him down as well. But he wouldn't let them. If they wanted to talk, fine, but he wasn't going to. No way. So he would have to lawyer up. Deny his involvement. Make sure that if this whole thing became public knowledge, he was well out of it. So he held up his hands. "Okay, if you want to talk to the cops, that's your prerogative, but I'm not talking."

"Marcus!" said Mel.

"I had nothing to do with this, all right?"

"You had everything to do with it! You handled the knife, and you handled those garden shears!"

"Only because you were all too weak," he snapped. "We promised we'd make sure justice was done for Allie, but when push came to shove, you all chickened out. So I did what had to be done, and if I hadn't, Allie's murderers would have walked away, scot-free. And I simply couldn't let that happen."

"Allie didn't deserve what she got," Edwina agreed. Of all the neighbors, she had always been the most fond of that girl. But then they all had adored Allie, who had been a bright light in the neighborhood. And with Marcus and Melanie being empty nesters and not coping very well, especially Mel, they had more or less looked upon Allie as a daughter, just as Edwina had treated her as the granddaughter she never had, and even Chris had seen Allie like a favorite sister. So when they had discovered that Chloe Fisher had murdered her beautiful girl in cold blood, with Mike helping her to cover up her tracks by disposing of the body in the lake, they had been furious. And then they had decided to get justice for Allie.

It hadn't been hard. They had all been so furious when they found out what happened. Mike had cracked, of course. The moment they confronted him with their suspicions about what happened to Allie, he had blamed it all on his wife, who had one of her attacks of crazy. They had known all about that since she frequently got that way. On the night of the murder, she and Allie had one of their epic rows that could be heard all around the neighborhood. They had even gathered in the street this time, concerned as they were for Allie and what her mother might do to her.

But before it came to blows, they had seen Allie race away on her bike, tears in her eyes. When they asked her what had happened, all she had to say was that she was leaving for good and that she had just told her mom and dad, and they hadn't taken kindly to the news. She had then raced off. Moments later, they saw Chloe get in her car and race after her daughter, which was when they knew things might quickly turn bad. Deadly, even.

They had gathered in the Fisher driveway to talk about what they could possibly do to protect Allie from her mother's insanity. But since they had no idea where she could have gone off to, they had been unsure what to do. But then Chloe had returned and assured her worried neighbors that everything was fine. She claimed that she and Allie had talked things through and that they had decided that for now, it was better if Allie stayed with a friend.

They hadn't believed her, especially Edwina, who could read the woman like a book. But it had taken them until the next morning to confront the couple. First Mike, who had admitted everything, and then also Chloe herself. Allie had driven down to the lake to cool off after her big fight with her mom, which was when Chloe had come upon her. Mother and daughter had picked up where they left off, only this time a physical altercation had followed. The fight had ended in the lake, with Chloe pushing her daughter's head under water until she stopped struggling. It was then that she realized what she had done and had returned home to get Mike. Together, they had gone back to the lake in the middle of the night, after their neighbors had gone to bed, and Mike had set out in a boat to dispose of their daughter's body. However, he hadn't done a good job because a fisherman had discovered her early the next morning.

Upon hearing the news from the Fishers' own lips, a righteous rage had run through the collected neighbors, and they had decided to take matters into their own hands. Mike had been first. That lily-livered, spineless piece of human misery had sniveled and begged for his life, so Marcus ended up having to chase him all the way across the road, where Jerry Garcia had graciously stopped the man's escape, giving Marcus the opportunity to finish the job. And he did so with relish. All for Allie. And then he had gone for Chloe.

Now he noticed that more neighbors had gathered. In fact, all of those who were present that morning had arrived and stood in the driveway. And for some reason, they all looked at him accusingly. Even the Garcias, who had been only too glad when he took matters into his own hands and delivered justice for Allie. As he stared back at his gathered neighbors, he could sense which way the wind was blowing. So when the police showed up and joined the gathering, he knew the game was up. Just like Chloe and Mike had ganged up on Allie, his neighbors had decided to gang up on him. Even his own wife gave him an odd look, as if he were some kind of vicious killer. But it was Chloe and Mike who were the killers, not him.

As he was led away in handcuffs, he wondered if perhaps Mel had a point. She had tried to stop him that day. But he had been so consumed with rage that nothing and no one could have stopped him. He even had to admit that he had enjoyed playing the vigilante for once.

CHAPTER 34

The barbecue in our backyard was in full swing, with our humans all gathered to enjoy the feast, and the feline contingent reposing on the porch swing in anticipation of those precious morsels that would soon be doled out. If the smell was anything to go by, it would be a feast to rival all other feasts, and frankly, I couldn't wait to dig my teeth in. But first, I had some explaining to do, as my friends were all eager to learn how I'd been able to crack this case.

"It wasn't hard," I told them. "Once I realized that it was the neighbors, and I knew where Bella was hiding, things simply fell into place."

"Things didn't 'simply' fall into place, Max," Brutus grunted. "You had to make them fit. So how did you hit upon the idea that it was the neighbors who had all ganged up on the Fishers?"

"Well, it was something Kingman mentioned when we first discussed the case with him," I said. "He used the word 'omertà,' code of silence, figuring the Fisher murders were a mafia hit. But this code of silence could just as easily have applied to what the Fisher's neighbors had agreed after Marcus Miller murdered Mike and Chloe. Allison Fisher was a very popular girl in that neighborhood. A ray of light, as Mrs. Malt described her. They all loved her, especially Edwina Malt, but also the Millers, and Chris Foster, who was only a few years older than Allison. So they all sympathized with the teenager when she got into fights with her mom, who presumably was suffering from some kind of mental disorder that had gradually become worse and worse over the years. Only that night, things really got out of hand, and Chloe ended up drowning her daughter in the lake."

"After Allison told her parents that she was moving to Texas to be away from them," Harriet added.

I nodded. "That's the straw that broke the camel's back. Chloe got into such a rage that she lost control of herself, and Allison ended up dead. That's when she and Mike tried to dispose of the body in a halfhearted way, causing a local fisherman to find the body. But Allison's neighbors already had their suspicions before the body was found in the morning, and so they all gathered and demanded answers from the girl's parents. And when Mike confessed what had happened, Marcus Miller decided to take matters into his own hands and exact revenge on the couple—with the full support of the entire neighborhood."

"Is that what Bella witnessed?" asked Harriet.

"Yeah, she saw the whole thing."

"But why didn't she say anything? Why protect her humans' killer?"

"Because she also adored Allison and wasn't particularly fond of the girl's parents for what they did to her. And what Chloe did to Bella."

"She pinched her."

"Well, she probably did more than just pinch her," I said.

We had talked to Bella, and she had admitted that Chloe

Fisher's disease had gradually become worse over the years, to the point that she often became physically violent with her daughter, her husband, and also their precious pet. So Bella didn't shed any tears when seemingly mild-mannered Marcus Miller decided to turn vigilante.

"Good thing Bella was adopted by Edwina Malt," said Harriet.

"Yeah, though it remains to be seen if the other neighbors, apart from Marcus, will be held accountable for their role in what happened that morning."

"But eventually Edwina told the police," said Brutus.

"She did. When confronted with the truth, she quickly told us the whole story. And then it was simply a matter of getting Marcus to confess. Which he did. Oddly enough, he didn't seem the least bit contrite. He claims he did what was right, and if given the opportunity, he would do it all over again."

"I think Marcus Miller is a dangerous man," said Dooley with a shiver.

"Yeah, there is something dangerous about him," I agreed. "He said he actually relished in the act of murdering his neighbors, which even shocked his wife. Instead of murdering the Fishers, they could have gone to the police. The Fishers would have confessed, and they would have been punished by a jury of their peers, not by Mr. Miller's particularly brutal campaign."

"I think you did well, Max," said Grace, who had joined us on the swing. "Even though it took you a long time to figure it out this time, didn't it?"

"Well, it was a complicated case," I said in my defense, "and also, I was distracted by the reality show business and this whole Cousin Beatrice thing."

"It would have been nice if that had gone through," said the toddler fervently. "I wouldn't have minded starring in a reality show. Like 'Toddlers & Tiaras?' Only we could call it 'Toddlers, Cats & Tiaras.' I think you would all look great in a tiara, especially Max, don't you?" We all stared at her in horror at the prospect, but then she laughed. "You should see your faces! I was only joking!"

"Oh, good," said Brutus. "Imagine the four of us wearing tiaras and being on national television. We'd become the laughingstock of the whole town!"

"I think I could pull it off, though," said Harriet. "I think I would look absolutely ravishing with a tiara."

"Yes, you could easily pull it off," said Grace as she gave Harriet a hug.

Harriet sighed. "Too bad Cousin Beatrice doesn't exist. I think this whole thing was a huge opportunity that we should have grabbed with both paws."

"We got abducted!" I said. "What opportunity?"

"Well, it's true that Sammie didn't handle that as well as he could have."

"His name isn't even Sammie! He is Kevin Thomson, and he's a reporter!"

Harriet shrugged. "Nobody's perfect, Max. But you have to admit he tried."

"He tried to expose Odelia! He wanted to show everyone that she can talk to us. And if he had succeeded, our lives would have been over."

"Or we could have all starred in a really interesting reality show," she insisted. "They could have called it 'Doctor Odelia Dolittle.' Or 'Odelia & Harriet.' Or even 'Harriet & Odelia.' Or why not simply 'Harriet?'" She smiled as the roseate dreams of what could have been drifted before her mind's eye. "One of these days," she promised us. "One of these days, I'll star in my own show."

I sincerely hoped she wouldn't, at least not if it ended up with all of us being made fools of on national television! But then, the last time Odelia checked, Kevin Thomson had been fired from the *Chronicle* for failing to deliver on his promise to expose Odelia and her family. He was training as a zookeeper now, possibly trying to reveal that they could all talk to the other zookeepers.

"At least our humans didn't start their own zoo," said Brutus.

"We've got enough of a zoo already," said Grace, voicing the general sentiment. "With four cats in the house, who needs a zoo, right?"

"Exactly," I said, happy to find myself in such sync with her.

Our meals had arrived, personally delivered by Odelia, and I, for one, was so grateful that I even gave her hand a lick. She rewarded me with a pat on the head and a whispered thanks for helping her and Chase crack this most challenging case. But then cracking cases is what I seem to do best. Other cats are good at catching mice, or ridding the home of other vermin, or keeping their humans company and reducing their anxiety and stress levels, and generally boosting their immune systems and overall health. But I solve mysteries.

Even Uncle Alec has started to appreciate my contributions, as evidenced by the fact that he came over and personally fed me a piece of his food. Though it could also have something to do with the fact that he was on a pre-wedding diet again.

"So when is Uncle Alec getting married?" asked Dooley.

"I'm not sure," I said. "Soon-ish, maybe?"

"Why does it always take so long for humans to get married, Max?"

"I guess it's a big undertaking, Dooley. A lot of moving parts."

"There's only two moving parts, Max. The bride and the

groom. All they have to do is say 'I do,' so how long can that take? Two seconds?"

"Yeah, but they want to do it right. In the right setting, in front of the right crowd, with the right priest, and hiring the right caterer for the wedding feast."

"Maybe they can do it in Vegas, like Odelia and Chase. That was fun, wasn't it?"

"Well..."

"Ooh, how was that wedding?" asked Grace. "Was it grand? It was, wasn't it?"

"Um..."

"It was a smallish affair," said Harriet, pursing her lips disapprovingly. She would have preferred if they held the wedding in Hampton Cove, inviting the whole town, as had been their initial plan. But apparently things had gotten a little out of hand, and in the end, they had more or less eloped and gotten married in Vegas, with only their immediate family present.

"Uncle Alec and Charlene will have a big wedding," Brutus assured her. "He's the chief of police, and she's the mayor. They have to throw a big do."

"Well, let's certainly hope so," said Harriet. "Cause I want a big wedding. I deserve a big wedding. I *need* a big wedding."

"Why do you need a big wedding, Harriet?" asked Grace.

"Because I'm a star, honey. And a star needs an audience."

"You're not... going to sing at the wedding, are you?" I asked.

"Of course I'm going to sing at the wedding! We're all going to sing at the wedding. Shanille and I are planning a special performance by cat choir, and it's going to be simply amazing. And then I'm going to sing my solo, and there will be a hush descending over the crowd, and then a raucous applause will break out!"

I could imagine the hush, but somehow I couldn't

imagine the applause. But I still gave her an encouraging smile. "That's great," I said. But judging from the look on Brutus's face, he wasn't fully on board with the plan.

"In front of all of Hampton Cove?" he asked. "You want us to sing in front of all of Hampton Cove, snuggle pooh?"

"Absolutely," said Harriet. "This will be the concert people will talk about for years to come. Decades, even! A once-in-a-lifetime event!"

Now that I could believe.

Dooley snuggled up to me and whispered, "Maybe we should elope, Max. So we don't have to get up there and make total fools of ourselves."

I grinned at this. "It's a deal, buddy. We'll make ourselves scarce on the day, and then later when we're asked, we'll tell them we fell asleep."

"Deal, Max!"

Harriet gave us a look of suspicion. "What are you two whispering about?"

"Nothing," I said. "Just looking forward to the big day."

"As am I," she said with a sigh of anticipation. "As am I."

THE END

Thanks for reading! If you want to know when a new Nic Saint book comes out, sign up for Nic's mailing list: nicsaint.com/news

EXCERPT FROM PURRFECT STAR (MAX 70)

Prologue

Jane Collins was walking along the quay and gazing out at the pretty boats and yachts that were moored in the Hampton Cove marina. It was a nice change of pace from being cooped up inside her home, where she had been hunched over her latest sewing pattern design. As a fashion designer, Jane had made quite a name for herself on sites like Etsy, selling her patterns to a great number of happy customers.

She wouldn't have minded boarding one of these yachts now, she thought as she looked upon their owners and passengers with a certain measure of envy. What she wouldn't give to be far away from Hampton Cove and to lie on deck, her hand trailing in the warm azure waters of some tropical paradise, cloud gazing and generally letting the world go by. It would certainly be a nice change of pace from what she was used to. As a mother of four, she knew what responsibility was, and had been taking care of her offspring and her husband Bert for so long now that she often forgot

EXCERPT FROM PURRFECT STAR (MAX 70)

that she also existed and also had a right to lead an exciting, wonderful and fulfilling life. Not that her patterns didn't give her a certain measure of satisfaction, and she certainly had received plenty of acclaim. Only not from the people who really mattered to her.

Which was why she was now walking along the marina and wondering about the choices she'd made. If she hadn't married Bert, for instance, but decided to somehow hang on to the other man in her life—in many respects the only man she had ever loved. She hadn't seen Robert in years, which hadn't stopped her from wondering if her life would have been different if they had stayed together. The man had certainly done very well for himself. So much so that he was being presented with an award by the Hampton Cove Chamber of Commerce. Ever since she had heard the news that her ex-boyfriend would be in town, she had felt unusually restless and wondered if she shouldn't leave town while he was there, almost as if she wanted to avoid him. On the other hand, she wanted nothing more than to clap eyes on the man who had broken her heart twenty-five years ago.

She paused for a moment in front of a particularly huge yacht that lay at anchor. Called the Aurora, she was sleek and gorgeous, and as Jane stood admiring her graceful lines, suddenly a person emerged on deck who looked vaguely familiar. But as she looked closer, she realized it was none other than Robert himself. He looked older, of course, but still as handsome as ever. He must have recognized her, too, for he did a double take, then slowly removed his sunglasses as he took her in. For a moment, the two ex-lovers simply stared at each other, then Jane saw that a single tear glistened in the man's eye, which is when she decided that maybe second chances existed after all, and she set her foot onto the gangway and stepped aboard.

EXCERPT FROM PURRFECT STAR (MAX 70)

Chapter One

Dooley had been snoring softly and was generally lost to the world when a strange sound made him prick up his ears and immediately return to full wakefulness. The sound seemed to come from somewhere nearby, and even though his first thought was that Max had produced the sound, upon further inspection he discovered that his friend was still sleeping peacefully by his side and hadn't moved an inch since they had fallen asleep together on the couch.

Dooley now lifted his head to take in the rest of the living room, turning his ears like antennae to scan his surroundings for a bead on the source of the sound, but try as he might, his ultra-sensitive ears could not pick up the sound again. Almost as if its design had been to bring him out of his peaceful slumber and then down tools, knowing its work was done and nothing more was required.

He yawned and stretched and decided to have a bite to eat, take a trip to his litter box, and generally do what cats do when they wake up and before they go right back to sleep. It wasn't too much to say that today was a day like most other days, with the marked difference that he didn't think the sun had been out in such splendor in quite a while. Hampton Cove had been blessed with plenty of rain lately, but now nature had apparently decided that enough was enough and had turned off the tap, bathing the world in a sunny glow for the first time in about a week. Nature was celebrating, for the birds were tweeting up a storm outside, the bushes and trees in the backyard all looked green and lush, and even the lawn looked as if it was in urgent need of a trim.

As he walked to the kitchen to see if his bowls were still filled to his satisfaction, Dooley noticed that the pet flap was gently swinging, as if someone had recently passed through there and had quickly left again when they became aware of

EXCERPT FROM PURRFECT STAR (MAX 70)

his presence. He didn't pay any mind to the strange phenomenon, figuring it was probably either Brutus or Harriet, the other two cats in their household. In due course he reached his bowls, and saw they still contained sufficient amounts of the good stuff, then made a beeline for his litter box for a tinkle. And that's when things turned a little weird. For when he arrived there, he saw that all the litter was gone, and not just in his personal litter box but also in Max's!

For a moment he simply stared at his empty box, scratching his head in wonder. That someone would have entered the house through the pet door to steal food from his bowl or drink his water was something he could have wrapped his head around, but why would anyone decide to steal his litter? As far as he knew, litter wasn't one of the major food groups. It wasn't nutritious, and possibly might even be harmful when ingested. And as he sat staring at his empty litter box, the front door of the house opened and closed, and moments later Odelia entered the kitchen, Grace on her arm, and he shared with her the gist of his complaint. Namely, that as a healthy grown-up kitty, he wasn't merely in regular need of sustenance but also of a receptacle to deposit the end result of his mastication and digestive processes.

Odelia, who clearly was as surprised as he was, promised she would look into the matter post-haste. At which point she simply walked out of the kitchen and left Dooley to his own devices, making him wonder if maybe he had failed to impress upon her the urgency of his request. Then again, he now realized she had looked a little distracted. In fact, she had only listened to him in a sort of half-hearted way and looked upon him as only a human could: her eyes seeing him, her ears hearing him, but her mind a million miles away. Almost as if she was dealing with problems of her own. Which was impossible, of course, for what could be more

EXCERPT FROM PURRFECT STAR (MAX 70)

important than a sneak thief who went around stealing litter from innocent cats?

Shaking his head at such a lack of cooperation, he decided to return to the couch and pour his lament into Max's ears. Max would listen. Max would understand what was going on here, and most importantly, Max would act and fix things. Max always did. Dooley didn't know how, but his friend was one of the great fixers in the world. Anything that was wrong, anything that went missing, any person or persons engaged in some form of wrongdoing, Max managed to right those wrongs and generally make things fine again. It was his greatest quality and what had made him Hampton Cove's very own feline Sherlock Holmes. And the great benefit of being friends with such a powerhouse of detection was that Dooley had access to that formidable brain at all times, which was both a blessing and a curse. A curse in the sense that a lot of people lay claim to Max's time, often causing Dooley's problems to take a back seat, just as they now had with Odelia. But also a blessing, for often Max only needed a single word to know how to proceed. But as he now approached the couch with the intention of uttering just this single word to place his friend in possession of the facts pertaining to the strange case of the missing litter, he saw that of his friend... there was not a single trace!

Somehow, in the five minutes that Dooley had been gone, Max had skedaddled. This made Dooley realize that the worst had happened—the thing he had feared the most for the longest time. Along with his litter, this mysterious sneak thief had also... stolen Max!

Chapter Two

Odelia wasn't feeling at the top of her game. Not only did she have several articles to finish and multiple looming dead-

EXCERPT FROM PURRFECT STAR (MAX 70)

lines hanging over her head like the proverbial swords of Damocles, but the woman who ran the daycare Grace attended had sent a message in the parents' WhatsApp group stating that due to a family emergency, the daycare would be closed for the next couple of days. This meant alternative solutions had to be found. Consequently, Odelia had paid scant attention to Dooley's litter lament and had immediately rushed out the door in search of her grandmother, hoping she would find the old lady next door.

She found Gran gazing intently at a caterpillar that had taken up position underneath a leaf on one of her precious rose bushes, seemingly transfixed on the bug. Observing the intensity with which her grandmother regarded the caterpillar, Odelia thought she wanted to zap it with her eyes, laser-beam it into oblivion. When Odelia cleared her throat to alert her of her presence, Gran redirected her gaze and, for a moment, something stirred within Odelia as she experienced the full impact of the old lady's baleful eye. But then Gran's gaze softened, and she even managed a smile. She probably had realized that Odelia was not a caterpillar.

"I've been keeping an eye on that one," she announced. "The old Vesta would have killed it dead, but the new Vesta wants to protect life. It's all about the preservation of life, you see. If we want to save the planet from destruction, we need to do it one caterpillar at a time."

"So you're going to let it eat your plants?" Odelia asked, surprised by this position.

"I didn't say I'm going to stand idly by and watch it destroy my lovely garden," Gran replied. "I said I'm keeping an eye on the little bugger. And if I see it take so much as one bite out of this here rose bush of mine, I'm going to pounce." She wagged a bony finger at the caterpillar. "Consider this your first warning, buster! One bite and you're out. Is that clear?"

EXCERPT FROM PURRFECT STAR (MAX 70)

"Gran, could you babysit Grace for me? Chantal at the daycare sent a message saying she's dealing with a family emergency and she has to close the daycare for the next couple of days."

"Oh, sure, honey," her grandmother said vaguely, her attention still riveted on the caterpillar, indicating she wasn't paying much attention elsewhere.

"Could you do it now?" asked Odelia. "I'm already late for work. I didn't see Chantal's message until I arrived at the daycare with Grace." She hadn't been the only one either. Three other moms had also arrived, surprised to find the daycare closed for the day, with a sign on the door informing them of Chantal's unexpected unavailability. It was highly unusual since Chantal Jones was a most conscientious and dedicated daycare owner, who loved the kids in her care as if they were her own. For her to suddenly close up shop was disconcerting, and when Odelia had more time to spare, she would definitely pay her a visit and see what was going on. She sincerely hoped Chantal wouldn't be inconvenienced indefinitely. Otherwise she'd have to find a different daycare, which might prove to be a tough proposition, as most of them were already full and didn't accept any new charges, especially a couple dozen of them.

"Sure, sure," said Gran with a wave of the hand. "Just leave it with me."

She would have pointed out that her daughter was not an 'it' but a 'she,' but then she knew it would be pointless. Once Gran had her mind set on something, it was pretty much impossible to shift it. So she placed Grace on the porch swing, kissed the top of her head, and hurried off again. Not only did she have several articles to write, but she also had an interview scheduled with the one and only Robert Ross, the multimillionaire actor whose yacht had arrived in the

EXCERPT FROM PURRFECT STAR (MAX 70)

Hampton Cove marina just the other day and had attracted so much attention.

Robert Ross was a local man who had left his home town many years ago to try his hand at different endeavors. According to local lore, he had worked as a handyman in a maharajah's harem, had competed in several boat races alongside the Prince of Brunei, and had even been the personal bodyguard of the Crown Prince of Jordan. He earned the man's eternal gratitude when he saved his life from an assassination attempt. During that particular act of heroism, he had sustained a gunshot wound to the stomach, which had been successfully remedied with the first pig-to-human stomach transplant in history, earning him an entry in the Guinness Book of Records.

After his checkered career, he had been selected as the next James Fox, and had now finished no less than six very successful Fox movies in a row, becoming one of the most popular actors ever to play that famous British spy. In other words, the man was a legend. When the rumor spread that his yacht was arriving in the marina, all of Hampton Cove showed up to greet him and give him a hero's welcome. Even Mayor Butterwick and Odelia's uncle had been there, although the latter's presence was for professional reasons only, to prevent anyone from trespassing or assaulting Mr. Ross aboard his vessel.

She hopped into her pickup and raced away, although the behavior of her aged Ford pickup was more akin to rattling away, as the noise the car made could probably be heard three streets over. She really should get a new one, but when she had asked Dan if he couldn't by any chance provide her with a company car, the editor had chuckled amusedly, pointing out that the newspaper trade was a dying industry and she was lucky to still have a job. Perks like company cars were not in the cards, unfortunately, and would never be as

EXCERPT FROM PURRFECT STAR (MAX 70)

long as she insisted on working as a reporter, as opposed to, say, an investment banker or a stock broker.

She arrived at the marina in due course and parked her car between a Porsche Cayenne and a Tesla, doing her best not to scratch either. She knew that these wealthy yacht owners didn't take kindly to scratches on their precious cars' paintwork. She hurried across the boardwalk to the quay where all the fancy yachts were moored. It didn't take her long to spot the Aurora, Robert Ross's personal yacht. It was easily the largest one in the small harbor. Recently, the marina had been completely redesigned and now featured a few luxury boutiques and fancy restaurants catering to the yacht owners who liked to visit these shops before heading into town. A more rustic experience awaited them there. If it were up to Charlene Butterwick, she would probably redesign all of Hampton Cove. However, she would face opposition from the locals, most of whom preferred things the way they were and had always been. Not that Odelia could blame them. Hampton Cove was a pretty pleasant town, even though it appeared a little sleepy to the more hip and cool segment of the tourist class.

She stepped onto the gangway to board the vessel, hoping Mr. Ross wouldn't be too upset that she was running late. But when she arrived on board, she was surprised to find that the yacht seemed to be deserted. Normally, for a man of Mr. Ross's stature, she had expected to encounter a small regiment of security personnel, personal assistants, and other crew members. However, she had boarded the vessel without being stopped, causing her forehead to wrinkle up in a frown. Having been on yachts before, she had some understanding of how they operated. Therefore, she headed to the bridge first, hoping to find a sign of life. The door was, of course, locked, which was understandable. As she walked along the deck, lightly placing her hand on the bulwark, she

EXCERPT FROM PURRFECT STAR (MAX 70)

traversed the vessel from bow to stern. To her disappointment, she found no trace of the famous movie actor.

She had reached the stern of the yacht and gazed up at the upper deck, where she knew a Jacuzzi and a small pool were located from the pictures she had seen. But there was still no sign of the boat's current resident. That's when she decided to climb the small metal ladder leading to the upper decks, hoping to find the actor sunbathing on the top deck, possibly having fallen asleep and forgotten all about their meeting. As she rounded the corner, she laid eyes on the small pool, a gorgeous azure blue in contrast to the beige wood of the deck, and noticed something floating in it. Moving closer, she saw that it was a person's body. Without a moment's hesitation, she jumped into the pool, swam with a couple of powerful strokes of her arms to reach the person, and started dragging the lifeless body back to the side of the pool.

Moments later, with a supreme effort, she hoisted the body out of the water and placed it face up on the decking. It was Robert Ross, and he appeared very much dead.

Chapter Three

When Dooley started messing about in the kitchen, and then Odelia walked in with Grace on her arm, I decided to desert my pleasant spot on the couch and go in search of more peaceful pastures to continue my nap in an uninterrupted fashion. I don't know about you, but I enjoy consuming my naps in one long session. So, I relocated to the rose bushes at the bottom of the garden, hoping to find them uninhabited by our housemates Brutus and Harriet, who often like to spend time there, engaged in their lovey-dovey activities.

I was in luck, as I found the location free of any lovers, whether pet or otherwise, and with a sigh of relish, I settled

EXCERPT FROM PURRFECT STAR (MAX 70)

down for the long haul. Or at least that was my intention. It soon became clear to me that it simply was not to be. Above me, an insect that looked vaguely familiar drew my attention to its plight, and before long, it was talking a mile a minute.

"Yo, Max," said the creature, which at this point I had positively identified as a caterpillar, "I've got a problem that's been giving me a headache."

I had the impression that the caterpillar was about to transfer this headache to me if I didn't get to take my nap, but nevertheless, I asked, "What is it?"

"Well, I've been hounded by this huge monstrous beast that seems intent on eating me, for some reason I can't possibly fathom."

"What beast, and why does it want to eat you?" I asked as I marveled at the mass of feet this creature had. I wondered how it never got them entangled. I guess there must be some kind of system in place.

"I'm not sure," said the caterpillar. "Oh, my name is Joe, by the way."

"Max," I said, "but then I guess you already knew that."

"Of course!" said Joe. "Who doesn't know the great Max? So the thing is, I've been hanging out here and minding my own business, when all of a sudden, this huge... thing homes in on me. Sometimes it's carrying a can and threatens to 'zap me to kingdom come.' Other times it tries to grab me and says it will 'turn me to mush.' Now, is that nice, Max? Is that kind? No, it sure ain't. So, I would like you to go and talk to this monster and tell it to lay off already. As far as I can tell, I never did anything to upset the beast, and still, it keeps hounding me!"

"What does this beast look like?" I asked.

"Like a scarecrow," said Joe, "but uglier."

"Okay, so an ugly scarecrow."

"Exactly. And it's not just me this scarecrow keeps harass-

EXCERPT FROM PURRFECT STAR (MAX 70)

ing. It's been happening to all of my friends too. It just goes around threatening us with destruction, and for what? Just because we happen to be alive? That's no way to treat any creature, Max, and it's definitely not the way I like to be treated."

"You wouldn't happen to have a name for this scarecrow, would you, Joe?"

The caterpillar thought for a moment, then finally nodded. "I think I've heard it being referred to as... Pesto?"

"Pesto."

"Yeah, must be a nickname." Suddenly, the caterpillar glanced up, and a look of alarm came over his tiny face. "Don't look now, but there it is. There, the monster comes!"

Ignoring Joe's strict instructions, I did look up and saw that Gran had approached the rose bush and was peering at it intently. She did have a can of some kind in her hand, I now saw, and I understood what was going on.

"Gran, don't use that bug spray on me," I told her immediately.

"Oh, Max," said the aged relative. "I didn't see you there for a moment. You wouldn't have seen any caterpillars, would you? It's just that my backyard has been invaded by the species, and they're eating all the leaves and destroying my precious plants and flowers."

Joe, who had taken to hiding underneath a leaf, now made frantic gestures in my direction to attract my attention. "Don't tell Pesto where I am!" he whispered loudly.

I shook my head as a sign that I wouldn't, causing his features to relax.

"No, I haven't seen any caterpillars," I lied to Gran. "But why are you trying to destroy them? You do know that eventually caterpillars become butterflies, right? And that they're a boon to any garden, a source of infinite pleasure with their colorful displays and graceful flights and flutterings."

EXCERPT FROM PURRFECT STAR (MAX 70)

"I don't care about any flutterings," said Gran, a bit more harshly than I would have liked. "All I care about is the survival of my flowers, and with all these voracious bugs hanging around, that won't be happening."

I eyed the can of bug spray with a curious eye. "I thought you were against the use of bug spray?"

She eyed the can with a look of wonder. "Oh, will you look at that? Who put that there?"

Gran had been going on about ethical gardening a lot lately, which as far as I could make out meant that she wasn't going to use any chemicals when she tilled her modest little patch with her claw rake, carefully removing weeds and making the soil ready to give of its best.

"Chemicals destroy everything and turn the earth into one big garbage dump. Isn't that what you said, Gran?" I asked.

"Of course, of course," she said. "Which is why I don't understand what this is doing here," she added, then proceeded to throw the can as far away from her as she could. It sailed across the hedge dividing our backyard from the next. There was a sort of loud thunking sound, followed by a soft yelp of pain, and moments later, Tex Poole, Gran's son-in-law, appeared in the opening in the hedge, rubbing his head and looking understandably irate.

"What's the big idea!" he cried. "Pelting me with cans!"

"That wasn't me," said Gran, even though she was the only one present.

"Of course it was you! Don't think I haven't seen you secretly using that spray on my flowers."

"Those are my flowers, and there's nothing secret about it. I was simply trying to get rid of those caterpillars."

"So you admit that you threw the can," said Tex.

"I will admit to no such thing!" said Gran, tilting her chin a little higher in a posture of indignation. "It was Max!" she said, pointing an accusing finger at me.

"A likely story," Tex scoffed. "Max couldn't throw a piece of kibble, let alone a can."

I would have told the doctor that I can indeed throw a mean piece of kibble, but since my opinion clearly wasn't required, I kept my tongue. Instead, I lay down again, watching the proceedings like one of those spectators at the US Open. I had a feeling this might prove extremely entertaining. I was even willing to postpone my precious nap to take it all in.

"Not only have you been using these horrible chemicals on my flowers, thereby poisoning the soil and endangering every species on the planet, but you threw that darn thing at my head!"

"That was an accident," said Gran quickly. "Max probably thought he was doing us a favor, but in his haste to get rid of the can, he failed to take into consideration that a certain person or even persons might find themselves in the flight plan of said can."

"You threw that can," said Tex, directing an accusatory finger at his mother-in-law. "Besides, why is it so important to get rid of those caterpillars? They're a very beneficial species, and besides, they turn into butterflies. You wouldn't murder a nice, innocent butterfly, would you?"

"Of course not, are you crazy? I would never raise a hand in anger at any creature, great or small. You know this, Tex. You know that I'm essentially a peaceable person and abhor violence of any kind." Tex actually rolled his eyes at this, and it wasn't that he was about to experience a fainting spell, but more to express his reservations about Gran's statement.

"Whatever," he said finally with a throwaway gesture of his hand. "But I'm confiscating this," he said, holding up the can. "And I better not see any more of this poison in my backyard."

"It's my backyard, too!" Gran cried indignantly.

But Tex had already left to return to his own backyard—having lost a few of his illusions but gained a tiny little bump on the head.

"That man drives me crazy," Gran grunted as she resumed her search for any trespassing caterpillars. "He always thinks he's right, even though half the time he's not."

"Shouldn't you both be at the doctor's office?" I asked. "Or have all of your patients been cured?"

"We're taking a day off," said Gran. When she saw I was staring at her with a sort of puzzled look on my face, she said, "Even doctors can take a day off, you know. It's hard work having to treat all of those patients, so from time to time, we need to take a break and not see any patients for an indefinite period of time."

"How long are you and Tex going to be out of commission?"

"Like I said, for an indefinite period of time."

"Is that your definite answer?"

She smiled. "Smart-ass."

ABOUT NIC

Nic has a background in political science and before being struck by the writing bug worked odd jobs around the world (including but not limited to massage therapist in Mexico, gardener in Italy, restaurant manager in India, and Berlitz teacher in Belgium).

When he's not writing he enjoys curling up with a good (comic) book, watching British crime dramas, French comedies or Nancy Meyers movies, sampling pastry (apple cake!), pasta and chocolate (preferably the dark variety), twisting himself into a pretzel doing morning yoga, going for a run, and spoiling his big red tomcat Tommy.

He lives with his wife (and aforementioned cat) in a small village smack dab in the middle of absolutely nowhere and is probably writing his next 'Mysteries of Max' book right now.

www.nicsaint.com

ALSO BY NIC SAINT

The Mysteries of Max

Purrfect Murder

Purrfectly Deadly

Purrfect Revenge

Purrfect Heat

Purrfect Crime

Purrfect Rivalry

Purrfect Peril

Purrfect Secret

Purrfect Alibi

Purrfect Obsession

Purrfect Betrayal

Purrfectly Clueless

Purrfectly Royal

Purrfect Cut

Purrfect Trap

Purrfectly Hidden

Purrfect Kill

Purrfect Boy Toy

Purrfectly Dogged

Purrfectly Dead

Purrfect Saint

Purrfect Advice

Purrfect Passion

A Purrfect Gnomeful

Purrfect Cover

Purrfect Patsy

Purrfect Son

Purrfect Fool

Purrfect Fitness

Purrfect Setup

Purrfect Sidekick

Purrfect Deceit

Purrfect Ruse

Purrfect Swing

Purrfect Cruise

Purrfect Harmony

Purrfect Sparkle

Purrfect Cure

Purrfect Cheat

Purrfect Catch

Purrfect Design

Purrfect Life

Purrfect Thief

Purrfect Crust

Purrfect Bachelor

Purrfect Double

Purrfect Date

Purrfect Hit

Purrfect Baby

Purrfect Mess

Purrfect Paris

Purrfect Model

Purrfect Slug

Purrfect Match

Purrfect Game

Purrfect Bouquet

Purrfect Home

Purrfectly Slim

Purrfect Nap

Purrfect Yacht

Purrfect Scam

Purrfect Fury

Purrfect Christmas

Purrfect Gems

Purrfect Demons

Purrfect Show

Purrfect Impasse

Purrfect Charade

Purrfect Zoo

The Mysteries of Max Collections

Collection 1 (Books 1-3)

Collection 2 (Books 4-6)

Collection 3 (Books 7-9)

Collection 4 (Books 10-12)

Collection 5 (Books 13-15)

Collection 6 (Books 16-18)

Collection 7 (Books 19-21)

Collection 8 (Books 22-24)

Collection 9 (Books 25-27)

Collection 10 (Books 28-30)

Collection 11 (Books 31-33)

Collection 12 (Books 34-36)

Collection 13 (Books 37-39)

Collection 14 (Books 40-42)

Collection 15 (Books 43-45)

Collection 16 (Books 46-48)

Collection 17 (Books 49-51)

Collection 18 (Books 52-54)

Collection 19 (Books 55-57)

Collection 20 (Books 58-60)

Collection 21 (Books 61-63)

Collection 22 (Books 64-66)

The Mysteries of Max Big Collections

Big Collection 1 (Books 1-10)

Big Collection 2 (Books 11-20)

The Mysteries of Max Short Stories

Collection 1 (Stories 1-3)

Collection 2 (Stories 4-7)

Nora Steel

Murder Retreat

The Kellys

Murder Motel

Death in Suburbia

Emily Stone

Murder at the Art Class

Washington & Jefferson

First Shot

Alice Whitehouse

Spooky Times

Spooky Trills

Spooky End

Spooky Spells

Ghosts of London

Between a Ghost and a Spooky Place

Public Ghost Number One

Ghost Save the Queen

Box Set 1 (Books 1-3)

A Tale of Two Harrys

Ghost of Girlband Past

Ghostlier Things

Charleneland

Deadly Ride

Final Ride

Neighborhood Witch Committee

Witchy Start

Witchy Worries

Witchy Wishes

Saffron Diffley

Crime and Retribution

Vice and Verdict

Felonies and Penalties (Saffron Diffley Short 1)

The B-Team

Once Upon a Spy

Tate-à-Tate

Enemy of the Tates

Ghosts vs. Spies

The Ghost Who Came in from the Cold

Witchy Fingers

Witchy Trouble

Witchy Hexations

Witchy Possessions

Witchy Riches

Box Set 1 (Books 1-4)

The Mysteries of Bell & Whitehouse

One Spoonful of Trouble

Two Scoops of Murder

Three Shots of Disaster

Box Set 1 (Books 1-3)

A Twist of Wraith

A Touch of Ghost

A Clash of Spooks

Box Set 2 (Books 4-6)

The Stuffing of Nightmares

A Breath of Dead Air

An Act of Hodd

Box Set 3 (Books 7-9)

A Game of Dons

Standalone Novels

When in Bruges

The Whiskered Spy

ThrillFix

Homejacking

The Eighth Billionaire

The Wrong Woman

Printed in Great Britain
by Amazon